Also by Sherri L. King:

Bachelorette

Chronicle of the Aware 1: Rayven's Awakening

Fetish

Midnight Desires, an anthology

Moon Lust

Moon Lust 2: Bitten

Moon Lust 3: Mating Season

The Horde Wars 1: Ravenous

The Horde Wars 2: Wanton Fire

The Horde Wars 3: Razor's Edge

Twisted Destiny, an anthology

What the critics are saying

"*PERFECT 10!* Hot enough to singe, RAVENOUS by Sherri L. King is one of the hottest paranormal books I've read this year...Ms. King does an excellent job of writing action scenes that seem to jump right off the pages, and love scenes that will cause every woman's heart to beat faster. A must read for lovers of paranormal romances and erotica, RAVENOUS by Sherri L. King will slake any reader's desire!"
- *Romance Reviews Today*

"*5 (out of 5) STARS!* I absolutely could not put this book down! There was so much action and love and hot, wet, sizzling sex packed into this book that the flow was incredible. My compliments to Ms. King on such a breathtaking work."
- *Timeless Tales*

RAVENOUS
An Ellora's Cave Romantica publication, May 2004

Ellora's Cave Publishing, Inc.
PO Box 787
Hudson, OH 44236-0787

ISBN # 184360535X

ISBN MS Reader (LIT) # 1-84360-229-6
Other available formats (no ISBNs are assigned):
Adobe (PDF), Rocketbook (RB), Mobipocket (PRC) &
HTML

Ravenous, edited by Jennifer Martin
Cover art by Darrell King.

RAVENOUS

Sherri L. King

For D

Many thanks to Nancy Adams for letting me borrow 'Squaker'.

Prologue

"Die, you son of a bitch—*hijo de puta*. Die! God, why won't you just die?" Cady Swann choked out as she buried her hands in the gushing black fount of the demon's chest. She searched out the giant beating heart of the beast, seeking to crush it and end the struggle at last. Her hands closed around the slippery black organ and she sank her fingers deep.

"*Die!*" The demon's clawed hands were digging into the flesh of her back, as the monster tried to make her join him in the throes of death. Cady's hands tore into the burning, putrid heart of the monster, sinking into flesh and sinew as if they were an over-ripe orange. Dark, sticky blood erupted from where her hands were buried, drenching the both of them as they struggled.

Bracing herself against the flailing form of her dying foe, she jerked back, away from the grasping claws at her back, and away from the open cavity of the creature's chest. Stumbling, she broke free at last of the creature's embrace, its black, oozing heart still clutched desperately in her fists. The skin of her back was aflame. It was an accompanying pain for the myriad other bruises she had sustained during the night's dark work.

Ignoring her wounded body's weakened condition, she immediately set to work on the still-pulsing organ in her grasp. She pulled upon the humming power that even now flowed like a raging torrent through her form, drawing upon the supernatural strength that she would need in order to fulfill her task.

With a strength that would have torn the limbs from a mere mortal man, she ripped the preternatural heart in two. The wet, tearing sound of it echoed through the moonlit wood. Pulling a small container of lighter fluid from her pocket, she doused the hideous heart, lit a match and set it ablaze.

The fallen form of her monstrous foe writhed and screamed as its heart was swallowed in the flames. Moments later with a gurgling, choking sound the creature was still at last. Dead without its beating heart.

She'd learned the hard way that to leave even a small bit of the heart still unburned would give the creature a chance to rise from its death. So it was after the heart had been reduced to a blackened husk of ash that she rose wearily from her crouch on the forest floor. With tired eyes she surveyed the scene around her.

Her night vision was excellent thanks to her "spooky talents"—a phrase she liked to use when referring to her enhanced senses. She could clearly see the fallen forms of two of the monsters as they lay dead about her. She would need to burn the bodies, she knew, to wipe away all traces of their existence. To hide the evidence of their evil.

No one must know these beasts existed. No one.

The two monsters she'd just killed brought the night's score up to five. And she still had four hours before dawn in which to find more of them to kill. She could feel the presence of more monsters out in the night. It was like an electric hum in her blood. Wearily, she released a long-suffering sigh.

It was going to be a long night.

Chapter One

Her hands were covered in the black muck of demonic blood. Her clothes were saturated in the thick, viscous substance, causing the fibers to harden and stick to her skin like glue. The job was getting more and more dangerous as time went on. If job it could be called, this strange nightlife she lived.

Unfortunately, if killing these monsters—vicious beings with preternatural strength and power—was a job, it sure didn't pay anything. Nor was it a career that promised much hope in the way of comfortable retirement. Hell, it was highly doubtful she'd even live to see retirement.

No. Killing the evil, murderous monsters was not so much a job for her as it was a calling. She'd been doing this for fifteen years now. Saving her town, maybe the world, from demonic infestation. Though admittedly she'd battled more and more often in recent months. This was her life.

One thing was certain. She had no intention of slacking off in her self-appointed duties any time soon.

As far as she knew the threat was limited to her hometown of Lula, Georgia. And for certain she was the only person who knew of the monsters' existence. Whether these creatures were an invading force of evil minions sent from hell to invade the world, or simply abominations who'd come to her town by chance, she didn't know. But no matter the answers to her endless questions, she had to fight the creatures. Or hundreds, perhaps thousands, of lives would be put at risk.

It was a thankless job, but she couldn't, in good conscience, shirk her duties. Lula might be a small, out-of-the-way railroad town, but it was her home. She cared about the simple, country-bred citizens. Knew most of them quite well. It was up to her to keep them safe.

Cady entered the darkened foyer of her small home situated on the outskirts of town. Her house was a humble one. Hardly the type of place you'd think a supernatural assassin would call home. The plain-fronted farmhouse had been built by her great-grandfather, and had been bequeathed to Cady in her grandmother's will upon her death, three years before.

She loved this house. It was her only safe haven.

It was a structure rich with fond memories. Memories of quiet summer days that smelled of sun-warmed crops growing in the garden. Of dancing in soft evening rain, and of tobacco smoke from her grandfather's ever burning pipe.

Her grandparents had raised her here after the death of her family, in the comforting shelter of their quiet home. She missed them both desperately. Her grandfather had died of a stroke when she was eighteen and her grandmother had died in her sleep nine years afterward.

She'd had many good years with her grandparents, true, but she still missed them with an aching heart. It was hard to be alone in so frightening and dangerous a world. Hard to acknowledge the fact that no one was waiting for her when she came home.

Cady breathed out a heavy sigh. Knowing that her memories would not leave her in peace this night, she leaned against the doorframe and looked into the darkness of her home.

She wondered, not for the first time, if this was all there was to life. *Her* life. Fighting almost nightly to save the innocent, then coming home alone to an empty house. Struggling to stay afloat financially and mentally. Only to have to do it all over again the next night.

She wondered if the monsters would suddenly stop coming. Maybe just as suddenly as they had first come that stormy night fifteen years ago. The night they'd killed her parents and little brother, Armand. The night she'd left her childhood behind and taken up the chase as if a gauntlet had been thrown, forever dedicating her life to the pursuit and destruction of the monsters.

Cady jerked back to herself. She had no time for such frivolous reveries. What she needed was a bath and a cup of hot, soothing tea. The sky outside was starting to lighten as the sun rose to bring the dawn. The monsters could not move about by day, so she and the people of Lula were safe...until the next nightfall. And the next. And the next.

* * * * *

Shoulders slumped and achy, Cady stepped further into the room. Even though the sky outside was brightening, little of the illumination reached beyond the windows of her home. Deep shadows swallowed the interior of the house but Cady didn't bother switching on a lamp to light her way. She was simply too tired to bother and too in need of a hot shower to waste the time.

It was a mistake. One she was not soon to forget.

From deep within the shadows, an arm struck out and wrapped itself around her neck. With a choked gasp, Cady struck out at the large form behind her. Satisfaction flooded her when she connected a solid blow against her attacker's head. She wasted no time, and brought her booted foot solidly against the instep of her assailant. As she heard the pained grunt from the form behind her, she thrust her elbow into a firm, muscled midriff and tried to squirm free of the restraining arm around her throat.

Instead of loosening his arm, her assailant tightened his chokehold on her, and brought his other arm around her middle. A large hand splayed wide across her stomach to better hold her still. She was jerked forcefully back against a hard muscled body. Her struggles were ignored, much like the buzzing of an insect.

The arm that encircled her throat suddenly contorted. Before her wide, startled eyes a glowing, blue-white blade erupted from the skin of her assailant's forearm. The electric glow illuminated most of the room. The blade arched out in a wicked curve from the muscular arm, to rest the deadly, winking point just below her chin.

"Do not move if you wish to live, *human*," a voice growled deeply into her ear.

Cady ceased her struggles abruptly — not because she feared that the man behind her would end her life — but because his voice compelled her to do his bidding. His voice was deep, but melodiously pure in tone, like the voice of an archangel. She suddenly had no will to struggle against him. In those heartbeats that followed the command of his magical voice she would have been willing to do anything for him.

Anything at all.

"With whom do you swear allegiance, mortal? Daemon or Shikar?"

"What do you mean?" she rasped out.

"Are you friend to the Shikar Alliance or to the Daemon Horde? Answer me, woman. Now, or I will bleed you out where you stand. You will be dead before you hit the floor."

"I swear I have no idea what you're talking about. And even if I did, why should I tell you? I mean—we haven't even been properly introduced," she quipped, before mentally cursing her smart-assed mouth. It was always getting her in trouble.

Fuck it. She was already in trouble.

Suddenly the hands that held her cruelly, roughly against her captor's hard form, released her. She was spun abruptly around, then pinned once more so that she faced him in the shadows. The arm sporting the wicked magical blade rested across her clavicle, once again placing the deadly point against her chin.

Cady's dark eyes flew up to the face of her captor, only to find it hidden in shadows too deep for her night vision to penetrate. Not even the bright glow of the blade at her throat pierced the shadows that swallowed her attacker's features. It was as if he controlled where the light fell, and he had no wish to reveal himself to her.

The hand that rested hot and firm upon her back, holding her tight against him, dug cruelly into the claw wounds on her back. It made her wince and fight against the urge to cry out. She felt the commingled ooze of her congealed blood and that of the monsters she'd killed squish between her back and his splayed hand.

"You have the Daemons' foul stench upon you, but you are virtually unharmed. How do you explain this, human? Do you dare consort with the Horde? Are you the Daemons' concubine, a wanton follower of their evil ways?" His fingers dug more forcefully into the wounded flesh of her back.

Cady's vision grayed as pain wracked her battle-weary body. She gritted her teeth against a scream but could not hold back an agonized gasp. She rallied her last reserves of strength and braced herself to fight. Her pain, fear and anger fueled the fires of her attack.

Taking her captor unaware, she swept her foot out and brought them both tumbling to the floor. Cady landed on top of him with a grunt. Wasting no time, she stabbed her hands into the exposed flesh of his throat, only to slam them with bruising force into the hardwood floor as he dodged her blow.

Using his substantially greater mass he turned them so that he towered over her as they struggled. But Cady was in full battle mode and it did not subdue her in the least. Using her knees, she kicked out against him, sending him flying over her head. Grabbing a dagger that she kept sheathed at her booted ankle, she whirled around to tackle her assailant as he struggled up from his position on the floor.

The man managed to shake her loose. Enough to stagger to his feet, at least. With mindless abandon she launched herself onto his back, sinking her teeth into his shoulder. She hung on for dear life as he tried to pry her off of him once more. Growling around the mouthful of flesh and muscle in her gripping jaws, she brought the knife to bear and sank it deep into his side. Hot wet blood spilled out over her hand before she was flung across the room. She had enough sense to brace herself for the impact that was sure to come—only to find herself suddenly plucked from her wild flight in the air by a hand encircling her throat.

He moved so fast! Faster than she could ever move, and she was an enhanced human. Or so she liked to think.

Her nails clawed the hand at her throat, leaving deep, weeping furrows behind. With a menacing growl her assailant brought her back against a wall. Her entire body was held inches above the floor by just the one hand clamped around her throat. Cady still could not see his face, but now she could see his eyes.

They were the same eyes she looked into each time she killed one of the monsters. His eyes were yellow-gold, with bold red rings around the pupils and irises. Though admittedly his eyes were clearer, lacking the bloodshot, glazed look that the monsters sported. In fact, they glittered like translucent jewels from beneath the longest, darkest lashes she'd ever seen.

This man was clearly different from a monster. His skin wasn't blistered and slimy, his blood appeared to be red instead of inky black, and he spoke plainly in English so that she could understand him. His voice was far too beautiful to belong to a monster. But his eyes were irrefutably alien and so like the monsters' that she wondered if he were a new breed of the hideous beings.

The thought left her cold and full of terror. If there were more enemies like the one she now faced, she feared she would never live to see another dawn.

In hopeless desperation Cady reached out before her, seeking out the soft, vulnerable flesh that shielded his heart. In her experience, every monster she'd ever faced had each possessed the same mortal weakness. The flesh of their chest cavities was like soft, over-ripe peaches, easily torn asunder to lay bare their hideous hearts. Her legs flailed over the empty space between them and the floor. With brutal force she struck out at his chest.

Only to bruise her knuckles against the hard, firm muscles that shielded his heart.

Oh God, she thought. *What is he?*

The assailant shoved her more forcefully against the wall, striking her head cruelly against it. Even as her vision dimmed from the blow to her skull she refused to cease her struggles. This must have angered him, because he raised his free hand and slowly brought a single finger to rest against her shoulder.

"Don't make me hurt you, woman. Cease your fight, and answer my questions; the dawn is almost upon us."

"*Fuck you*," she choked out, lashing out with her fist. She aimed for his nose, but he managed to evade her blow so that it glanced off of his cheekbone instead. Regardless, she felt no small amount of satisfaction knowing that he would at least bear a bruise for her efforts.

"I'm not really in the mood, just now," his beautiful voice bit out, just before a blue-white blade shot out from the tip of his finger. It stabbed cleanly through the muscle of her shoulder, like a hot knife through butter.

Cady screamed as the searing pain in her shoulder registered to her brain. Her assailant loosened his hold so that the weight of her body rested on the blade that ran straight through her shoulder and beyond into the wall behind her. She was suspended on that keen and wicked pain as he bent forward to breathe softly into her face.

"Do not make me hurt you further, little one." Was his voice gentler? Did she detect some small regret at his cruelty staining the dulcet tones of his voice? Or was she so consumed by pain that she was imagining things?

"Answer my questions, and your suffering will end. Are you friend or foe to the Shikars? Speak the truth or I will know you lie."

"I...I...it *hurts*," she whimpered. She could not think beyond the pain of the bright blade that pierced her flesh. Later, probably, her show of weakness would shame her. But not now. Now she wanted nothing but to escape from the horrible pain.

"I know it hurts, but you would not cease your struggles. I did not intend to come here and visit harm upon you. I merely wanted answers—answers which you still have yet to give me." His last words were gritted out and he twisted his finger, causing the blade to bite more cruelly into her tender flesh.

"God! Please!" she screamed as the pain unbelievably intensified. "I'll tell you anything—*anything*! Just...*just stop*."

"With whom do you side? Shikar or Daemon?"

"I—I don't know any Shikar or Daemon," she managed. It surprised her that she could talk at all. Her body had begun to shake and tremble with the waves of agony.

"You speak the truth...and yet you do not. You smell of the Daemons. You are covered in their filth." His intense, burning eyes blazed a trail down her form.

"You mean the monsters?" Her thoughts were a jumble, but she managed that bit of reasoning before she once more gave in to the pain that drove her. She moaned and writhed against the blade in her shoulder, seeking to keep her weight from bearing down so heavily upon it.

She braced herself by holding onto his wrists with both hands. He certainly was strong. His arm didn't even tremble under her weight. Their breath met between them—his deep and calm, hers shallow and rapid. He brought his free hand up to lay it softly over hers. She wondered if he meant his gesture to be comforting. Oddly enough, it did serve to comfort her a little...until another wave of pain swept her up once more.

"Daemons, monsters, hell-spawn—they are the things whose blood now soak your clothing," he breathed deeply as if scenting some fragrant perfume on the wind, "as well as your own."

"I killed seven of them tonight." Her voice shook with the effort of biting back her cries of pain. "I'll kill you as well and break even with my record of eight...just give me a second to catch my breath, okay?" She knew her boasting words were foolhardy in the extreme, but she couldn't help it. More than the pain, she hated being at his mercy, and the only way she could lash out was with words.

"Such brave boasts from so small a mortal woman. So you are no friend to the Daemons. You've met them in battle and triumphed. But you are a woman, not a Shikar warrior. How can this be? I sense the truth of your words, but how is it possible? You are...*human*." He spat out the last word as if it were some vile epithet.

"It hurts...hurts so bad," she whispered weakly. She could no longer focus on his words, but she was far beyond caring. Her head was swimming, her brain going fuzzy. She hated her weakness, but she'd never felt such an invasive pain before. In all her years of battling against the forces of evil, she'd never before sustained such a debilitating and painful injury.

"I will leave for now. The dawn has arrived. But I will be back—and we will talk. You have caught the attention of my people, and we will have the answers we seek from you." He pulled the blade from her shoulder, catching her to him as she fell.

"Until we meet again, woman." He breathed the words at her ear, making them a promise. A threat.

Her world became darkness, as she fell into a swoon to escape the pain.

Chapter Two

Obsidian ran his hands over his bleary eyes. He was tired and weary after the night's events, looking forward to finding his rest for the night. First however, he must go before the Elder and make his report concerning his altercation with the mortal woman. This was a meeting he did not anticipate attending in the least.

He should not have hurt her.

Guilt washed over him. He hadn't intended to harm the woman, but his anger at her possible involvement with the Horde had driven his actions. He'd lost control. For some reason he couldn't fathom, the thought that she might be aiding and abetting his enemies had felt like a personal betrayal. It was a reaction that he could not explain—even to himself. He had almost *wanted* to hurt her. To make her feel the pain that *he* felt over her seeming choice of alliances.

But then he had discovered that she was innocent of any wrongdoing. Her confusion alone over his questions concerning the Daemons should have been enough to convince him of her innocence. It had only served to anger him more, for it proved beyond any doubt that she was a mere human. To his mind she therefore had placed herself recklessly in the path of the invading Horde with her heroics. The little fool.

No human had the power to stand and win against a Daemon.

Oh yes, he and his allies had heard of her victories against the evil scourges that managed to evade the

Shikar warriors. Her legend had spread far and wide amongst the Shikar Alliance. But legend — *myth* — it was surely, for no Shikar warrior had ever encountered a mortal with the strength or cunning to outmatch even the weakest Daemon. It just wasn't possible.

Was it?

After this morning's struggles with one Cady Swann, mortal woman, Daemon Hunter, he just wasn't so sure of anything anymore. He'd never been bested in battle, but somehow that slip of a woman had charged past his defenses as if they were naught. She'd actually succeeded in wounding him!

She'd marked him with her sharp teeth, a deep ugly bruise at his shoulder, and she'd nearly broken his cheekbone with her fist. It had taken great concentration to mentally heal the knife-wound in his side after he'd left her. Not to mention the other various bruises he'd sustained while trying to subdue her.

He'd elected to leave the bite-wound unhealed, as a reminder that he was not invincible. To remind him of his ill treatment of Cady. But deep down, on some primal level, he knew that he'd left the bruise because he relished bearing her brand upon his flesh. He wondered fleetingly what it would be like to have her mark him thusly in a fit of passion, instead of rage.

Bah! Such thoughts were unlike him. Where was his warrior's honor? It lay wounded at the mortal woman's feet. That's where.

His humiliating wounding at her hands had fueled the fire of his temper. He'd warned her not to struggle against him, but she had paid him little heed. She should have known better than to defy the most feared warrior of the Shikar Alliance.

But now that he could repent his actions at leisure, he wished he'd refrained from retaliating against her using his foils. He'd known that the foils would inflict great pain upon her. It was, after all, their very purpose. His species had evolved in such a way that the foils—deadly retractable blades embedded deep within their bones—excreted a fatal poison into the wounds of a foe. The poison killed slowly, so slowly in fact that the victim could well die from the pain of it long before the poison reached the heart.

He had, of course, only allowed a tiny amount of venom to seep into Cady's wound. It had taken great amounts of mental control, but he had managed to keep her from feeling the brunt of the foil's poisonous bite. When she'd passed out in his arms, he'd promptly neutralized the venom and healed her wound, not wanting her to die from the poison. Not wanting her to feel any more pain due to his rough treatment of her.

He'd removed her shirt to see to her injuries, and it was then that he'd noticed the vicious claw marks that ran down her back. The wounds had clearly been inflicted by a Daemon, for they'd already begun to fester and boil. He saw to the healing of those wounds as well as the other scrapes and bruises that dotted the rest of her lush body. He'd left no portion of her body unexplored, seeing to even the smallest of injuries.

She'd been so beautiful in her quiet repose, her caramel skin soft and supple under the healing touch of his hands. Her flesh had felt like warm, living silk beneath his hands. If she'd been awake he would have wanted to spread her out on the bed and gift her with pleasure the likes of which she'd never known.

Where had that thought come from? He shook his dark head, sending his long hair flying. There was no way he was growing soft for a human, surely. He couldn't stomach the idea. Oh sure, he'd rut with a human woman any time. Human women were often delectable fucks. But that's all it was—a fuck. No softer feelings involved, no tender words or vows.

Just the hard, wet slap of flesh on flesh in the race toward mutual ecstasy.

Turning a corner in the deep bowels of the underground temple-city, he was jerked from his thoughts as he caught sight of Tryton, The Elder.

"Obsidian, how fares the little warrior?" Tryton asked, his voice deep and resounding through the stone corridor.

So it was to be this way, was it? Obsidian could almost hear the censure coating The Elder's voice. He suspected Tryton already knew the answer to his question, but wanted to hear what Obsidian had to say nonetheless. He debated his answer as they turned to walk in the direction of the warriors' apartments, nestled within the heart of the temple-city.

Tryton was a large man, almost as large as Obsidian was at six-foot-ten inches. And though he was an elder member of the Shikars, he in no way looked as if the title was appropriate. His face was ageless, neither young nor old. By a human's standards he looked perhaps close to forty years, until one looked into his eyes.

It was his eyes that gave him away. The title of Elder fell to him because he was a member of the Council, a group of the wisest Shikars. Tryton was often called The Elder because he was the leader of the Council, the oldest and wisest of them all. No one knew his true age but there were rumors that he was over two thousand years old. Looking now into Tryton's bright yellow eyes, full of limitless secrets and knowledge, Obsidian could well believe the rumors.

"My meeting with the mortal did not go as planned, Elder. She was…difficult."

"Will she side with us against the Horde?"

"I didn't get that far in my interrogation." Obsidian almost cringed as he admitted his defeat over such a minor task.

"Interrogation? You were sent to speak with her, not intimidate her. The human known as Cady Swann is no criminal to be interrogated. She should be heralded as no less than a hero amongst us for her many victories against the Horde."

"We did not know for certain if the rumors were true," Obsidian bit out in his defense.

"No, my friend, *you* were not certain—but I knew the truth behind the stories. Cady is a human, yes, but she is possessed of great psychic gifts. These gifts have stood her in good stead as she battles against the Horde, and they would stand us in good stead if she would but join our ranks."

Obsidian stopped walking and clenched his teeth against the urge to roar. He managed to ask in clipped tones, "Why didn't you tell me you knew the stories to be true? I thought her allegiance was in question—as well as her conquests on the field of battle."

Tryton raised a golden brow. "Her allegiance has never been in question, Obsidian. She fights the Daemons on an almost nightly basis. Her kills number in the hundreds. *Of course* she is on the side of good. But would she join with us—that was the question I meant for you to put to her."

Obsidian growled and ran a hand over his scalp, dislodging the leather thong that held his hair in place at his nape. Midnight-black waves of silken hair spilled loosely about his shoulders and down to his waist. His amber eyes flashed and sparked in agitation.

Tryton saw Obsidian's fit of pique and closed his eyes on a weary sigh, "Please tell me you didn't bully her on your first meeting, Obsidian."

"How was I to know your intentions? You told me to seek out the Swann woman and to find what her intentions were regarding the Horde. I didn't know you meant for her to join with us."

"Tell me what happened. Leave nothing out."

A few moments later, Tryton tried not to smile as his most trusted and loyal warrior recounted the events of the night. Obsidian gesticulated angrily, his words and actions volatile as he recounted the mortal woman's attack upon his person. Obsidian seemed shocked and almost insulted that the woman had *dared* to defy him in such a manner. Tryton found the development interesting—and promising. His goals for the outcome of this night's work became two-fold. Not that he would ever admit that to the angry warrior before him.

"So essentially what you're telling me is that you've likely insulted this woman to the point where she won't have anything further to do with us?"

"I'll take care of it. If you want this...*human* to join us then join us she will." Obsidian threw back his exceptionally broad shoulders in an arrogant, proud stance.

"I do not want her forced," Tryton warned in a tone that brooked no arguments.

"Consider the matter resolved, Elder. I will not force her, but rest assured, she *will* join us."

"See that she does, Obsidian. See that she does."

Chapter Three

Cady shot upright in bed, wincing at the protests her stiff muscles made over such an abrupt movement. It took her but a second to realize that she should be feeling quite a lot more discomfort than merely stiff muscles. She reached back to feel for the furrows at her back, her shoulder moving painlessly when it should have been too damaged to do so, and it was then that she realized that her wounds had miraculously healed.

And that she was totally nude.

"*Hijo de puta.*" Son of a bitch, she muttered in Spanish under her breath. Though she wasn't exactly *angry* that her attacker had seen her in the nude, she wasn't too happy about it either. He had, after all, healed her injuries and put her safely to bed. It was his only saving grace as far as she was concerned.

But if it hadn't been for his invasion of her home and subsequent rough treatment of her she wouldn't have needed his assistance with her injuries in the first place. The most serious injury she'd sustained the previous night had been the deep furrows in her back. But a soak in bath salts and some rubbing alcohol would have kept the wounds from getting too infected. Probably.

Glancing at her bedside alarm clock she groaned. It was after eleven in the morning and she was due at work by noon. She threw back the bedcovers and jumped from her bed to get ready for the day ahead. Her nightlife didn't allow for much leeway in terms of her business hours. Especially during the winter months, when sunset came earlier than at any other time. But she had a job that she enjoyed, and it paid the bills, which was really all she cared about in terms of her daytime career.

She worked in a local bookstore from twelve to six, Monday through Saturday. Not a full-time career, but she didn't really have time for one. Her hours at the bookstore allowed her to be ready every nightfall to meet any monsters that should come her way, which was the most important thing. Though her schedule didn't allow for much free time, she was able to get about four hours of sleep each night, which was really all she needed.

She had more important things to do besides waste her time sleeping.

Rushing through a shower, she growled at the stubbornly clinging bits of dried demon blood on her skin and hair as she hurried. Her skin was rose-red when she stepped from the shower, but it was free of any traces of blood and grime. She hurriedly threw on a pair of black slacks and a sleeveless knit turtleneck. It was quick work for her to secure her hair in a tight braid, as she'd been doing it every day for years. Jauntily, she tossed the thick rope of hair over her shoulder and finished preparing for the day ahead. She'd never been overly enthusiastic about fussing over her appearance.

Cady had always been more practical than vain. It was something her Puerto Rican grandparents had never fully understood. She remembered they always chalked it up to her being a tomboy. After all, she'd taken judo and karate lessons for years, not to mention that she was an active member of their local shooting range. Things like martial arts and weapons training were masculine pursuits in their eyes.

They hadn't known she'd been training for real combat. Her grandparents had never known that from the age of sixteen she'd been sneaking out of her window at night, armed to the teeth, honing her psychic skills and tracking monsters when they were near.

Grabbing her daily essentials she made for the door, and prepared to act like a normal human...if only for a few hours.

* * * * *

"I was just telling my Henry the other day, 'that girl needs to get herself a man and settle down to have some kids'..."

Cady let the never-ending drawl of Maple Harris's voice fade into the background as she scanned the area for some avenue of escape. One of the drawbacks of growing up in such a small town as Lula was that everyone knew everyone else's business. Or thought they did. The older people, such as the seventy-year-old Maple, often took it upon themselves to meddle in other people's lives. *Especially* when it involved matchmaking of any sort.

"You're not getting any younger, Cady. If you don't find a husband and start a family soon you'll end up an old maid."

"I'm only thirty, Mrs. Harris. Nowadays people don't see that as an age even close to placing one 'on the shelf' as it were. Besides, it's kind of hard to meet any interesting guys in the social Mecca that is Lula."

Cady's sarcasm was lost on the older woman. "What about Imogene and Spurgeon's son? He's not much older than you, and a hard worker from what I hear. Looks as though he'd be a decent husband and provider for any children ya'll might have."

"Jonny *Buckshot* Greenaway? Not a chance. He's forty-five with a comb-over and a potbelly, and he only works as hard as he does because he needs the money to support his drinking and gambling habits. No thanks. I'd rather die an old maid."

"What about Redd Little? We all saw how well ya'll got on last fall. Me and Belle were sure you two were headed for the chapel." Belle was Maple's best friend, and together they made for the busiest gossips in town.

"We went out twice, both times to Rabbit Town Café for a burger and fries. We weren't dating, we were just hanging out. We've been friends since high school. *Friends* mind you, nothing more," Cady defended.

"You just didn't give him enough of a chance. And now he's out dating that upstart city girl from Atlanta."

"I met her," Cady sighed, more than weary of the conversation already. "I thought she was a nice girl. Redd needs a nice girl, someone who won't walk all over him. He's too laid back for an aggressive kind of woman."

"Like *you*, you mean? If I told your Granny once, I told her a million times. She let you run wild after your family died in that storm, may the good Lord rest their souls, and now you're too old and set in your ways to change. How will you meet a good man to marry if you don't start…" Maple launched into her favorite lecture regarding the merits of being a meek woman and settling down with a big, braw man.

Cady had heard the same lecture since the day she'd turned eighteen, from Maple Harris and the myriad other busybodies of the town. It was always the same. People thought Cady was just too wild and free-spirited, and in their eyes, if she would just settle down and raise a passel of kids, she would be tamed enough that they wouldn't have to worry about her anymore.

And worry they did, for the people of the town were well-meaning enough, if a bit judgmental. Cady knew they meant to see her happy. The problem was that her idea of happiness and their idea of happiness were two very different things altogether.

She would be happy, well and truly, to not find herself fighting supernatural monsters on a regular basis. What had her strange visitor the night before called them? Daemons. The Daemon Horde. Cady felt the title was more than appropriate for the hideous beasts.

As they had many times throughout the long hours of the day, Cady's thoughts once again strayed to her visitor from the previous evening. For some strange reason she couldn't yet comprehend, she no longer thought of him as her attacker. True, he had invaded her home, fought with her, and interrogated her. But she couldn't bring herself to completely hate and fear him after he'd so helpfully seen to her wounds before he'd left her.

It was obvious that he hadn't wanted to be out after dawn—for reasons she didn't care to dwell on at the moment—and it surprised her that he'd stayed to see to her care while she'd been unconscious. She wondered just how long it had taken him to heal her wounds, and just how he'd gone about doing it. One thing was for absolute certain. He hadn't healed her in any conventional manner.

He'd said that they would meet again, and Cady couldn't help but wonder how soon he intended to see his promise fulfilled.

Chapter Four

Cady swept the folds of her black trench coat around her and gathered her things in preparation to leave her shift. The bookstore would stay open until nine, and though her employer often wanted her to extend her hours to closing time, she always left promptly at six. She had more important matters to see to besides getting more hours on her paycheck.

She knew the townsfolk saw her as something of an oddity, but she didn't fight evil every night to gain the respect of her peers. Hers was a thankless job, but one she felt was more important than social acceptance could ever be. In good conscience, she knew she would never be able to set aside her self-appointed duties. So she tried not to dwell too much on the many personal costs demanded by her strange lifestyle.

The weather was already turning warm outside. Though it was only February, the southern spring was coming early. So when Cady stepped outside the shop after waving goodbye to her co-workers and boss, she immediately felt overdressed in her long coat. But wear it she must, for the monsters had been busy recently, and deep within the concealing folds of her coat lay nestled a small arsenal should she have need of it. Though it was early yet for the Daemons to be out and about, she liked to feel prepared.

It would be a little while longer before sundown. That gave Cady just enough time to go home and change into her usual monster hunting attire, and to gather what weapons she could easily carry. To prepare herself mentally for the battles she was sure to engage this night.

And to feed her cat, Squaker.

* * * * *

She felt him just as she stepped into the house. Her extrasensory perception clamored in alarm before she tamped down on the panicked feeling. This time she didn't give him the advantage of surprise. Instead, she whipped out her Browning and pointed the muzzle of the gun in the direction she knew he was standing.

"Let's cut to the chase, Mister. What are you, who are you, and what do you want from me?" In the growing shadows she saw him shift, his muscles moving with a barely suppressed violence. The sun was setting outside, and Cady was struck with the thought that they had come almost full circle from the night before.

"Do you feel protected behind your mortal weapon?" he asked.

"Yeah, pretty much." Cocky? Her? *Nah.*

"Then I shall let you keep it...for now."

"You're a real arrogant piece of work, do you know that? But it seems I'm the one holding the gun, which means you have to answer my questions this time around."

"Are you sure you're ready to hear my answers, mortal?"

"I'm going to count to three and if you haven't answered me by then, I'm going to empty my clip into your ass. One..."

"Be warned, mortal. Your cocksure words could stray into the realm of the foolhardy. I have little patience for the bravado of your kind."

"Two…"

"You wish to know what I am? Very well, I will tell you, but only because it suits my own ends to do so. I am a Shikar. I am a respected and feared warrior of that great and ancient race. I am Obsidian, son of Lance — the greatest warrior the Shikar have ever known. Can you boast of so great a lineage, woman?"

"That doesn't answer anything for me, and you know it. What is a Shikar?"

"We are the Guardians against the Horde. We are all that stands between their world and yours. We keep mortals and immortals alike safe from the tide of evil, keeping the Daemons from entering your dimension."

"You're not human."

"Indeed not. My race is an ancient and powerful one. We've been here since the beginning. We stand watch at the Gates between the worlds, keeping order and balance. Without us there would be nothing but chaos and death."

Cady's gun wavered. What was he saying? Her mind wanted to disbelieve him, struggled to, but what he said made sense on many levels. She firmed her grip on her firearm, squaring her shoulders.

"Well you Shikars obviously haven't been doing too good a job *protecting* lately. For the past fifteen years I've seen a steady rise in the monsters' activity. It's no picnic cleaning up after you guys, you know."

"Which brings me to your last question — what I want. I want you to join with us in our battle against this newest surge of Daemonic activity."

"Give me a break. Last night you almost killed me because you thought I was your enemy. Now you want me to team up with you? I'm not completely dense—I can hear your derision when you speak of my humanity. My mortality. What's made you change your mind so quickly?"

"I haven't changed my mind. I have no respect for your kind. You live off the fruits of our labors. You go through life unaware of the constant threat to your safety. Your very existence. All you care about are your material possessions, your petty successes, your station in human society—"

"Hey! Not everyone is like that, and you certainly can't include me in your prejudiced view of humankind. I've spent my entire life practically shunned by my peers due to my penchant for Daemon hunting. I don't do this for material possessions, or popularity. I do it because no one else will."

"I apologize, of course." He bowed at the waist, and even in the twilight Cady could see his eyes flash. Whether in amusement over her outburst, or irritation that she'd reprimanded him, she couldn't say.

"And you're absolutely right," he went on to say. "You are not like these other humans. You say you hunt Daemons because no one else will—I say *no one else can*. I've never heard of a mortal that could face a minion of the Horde and live to tell of it, much less leave the struggle triumphant. I salute you for your courage and prowess in battle. I'm sorry if my words offended you."

She didn't know if he was serious or merely humoring her. She assumed the latter. "Don't patronize me. Good grief, are you always this annoying? No! Don't answer that," she warned when he made a move to speak.

"You'll just say something flippant and piss me off. Remember, I'm the one holding the gun, so just answer my questions without getting cute—"

Her words were cut off abruptly as she felt a stinging blow to her arm. Then the Browning was wrenched cleanly from her hand. She looked to the place where her adversary had been standing, and saw the glint of her gun barrel as it was pointed squarely at her.

She hadn't even seen him move.

"*Son of a bitch*," she growled.

"Now, it would seem that I am the one holding the gun, *human*. Perhaps now you should show me a bit more respect."

"When hell freezes over. Maybe." She sighed, and relaxed her stance, crossing her arms negligently over her stomach, hands resting under the lapels of her coat. "Look, I'm tired of arguing with you. Can we cease with the posturing and get on with it? In case you haven't noticed, nightfall is upon us, and I have work to do. Tell me exactly what it is you want from me."

"Shall I set your human weapon aside, so that we may speak as comrades?"

"Sure, I don't see why not." Would he do it, she wondered? Was he that stupid…or that skilled?

She eased her hands closer to the hidden gun holstered at her side. It was a good thing she'd donned the loose shoulder harness in her car before entering the house. She'd learned her lesson the night before, knowing she'd need every trick she could devise to use against this man should he show up uninvited in her home again.

He slowly laid the gun down on a nearby table. Holding his hands up, palms out in front of him in a position of truce, he backed away from the weapon. He settled himself back into the shadows and seemed to await her next words.

It was all the opportunity she needed.

The gun hidden at her side fell into her hand as if by magic, and she charged toward him, weapon at the ready. She didn't want to use the gun. So she used all of the speed she could muster, moving faster than any normal human eye could discern, hoping to take him to the floor and subdue him.

She just wasn't fast enough.

Within the space of two breaths she was stopped mid-flight—her gun plucked once more from her hand. She was thrust back by a hand at her chest, and she fell upon the hardwood floor with a thud. Her body was jarred in the rough landing, but it was the wall that landed on top of her that stole her breath from her.

The wall was his body, a heavy, solid mass. Before she even had time to catch her breath, he had insinuated himself between her legs. His hips rested in the cradle of her thighs and his chest held her to the floor. He secured both her arms in one strong hand and gripped her chin with the other so that she looked him squarely in his strange, glowing eyes.

She was effectively pinned, unable to move.

"I just wanted to talk with you. But you had to do it the hard way."

"I do everything the hard way. I've been told I don't know any better." She gritted her teeth against her humiliating situation, trying and almost succeeding to sound flippant.

He seemed to be enjoying her discomfort. In more ways than one. She could feel the hardness of his erection pressed against her and wondered what was to come next. She saw his eyes flare and glow, sparks seeming to shoot deep within their golden depths. A stray shaft of moonlight fell across them and she caught her first clear glimpse of his face.

Her heart nearly stopped beating in her chest.

Chapter Five

He was gorgeous! Beautiful. Sex personified.

His face was the fantasy of every woman's wet dreams. He had flawless skin, bronzed and masculine. With a proud, aristocratic nose and a mouth that was surely sculpted by a cosmic master artisan with but one purpose in mind. The creation of a sex god. His mouth alone made heat pool low in her belly, setting off her libido like a torch to dry kindling.

His hair was his crowning glory. Though it was pulled back away from his face, she could tell it was long and thick. It was black, so deeply black that it seemed to swallow up all the surrounding light into its depths. It glistened like glass, so shiny that the black hue of it would probably appear blue in a strong light. She sighed. She was a sucker for a man with good hair.

"*Carajo*," she breathed in appreciation.

Obsidian saw her reaction to his appearance and smiled to himself. For some reason her appreciation of his charms pleased him more than it should. It was true that human women often thought him pleasing to look upon, but until now his physical appearance had only been a means to an end. A way to lure women into his arms and into his bed.

But now, looking into Cady's dark, human eyes, he felt something close to pride that she found him attractive. Something close to triumph.

"You speak Spanish?" he asked in kind, noting her stunned expression with some satisfaction. Shikars could speak nearly every human language fluently. They were born with the ability and it was a gift that came very much in handy while amongst humans.

"A little. My father and grandparents were from Puerto Rico," she gritted out.

Closing his eyes, he breathed deeply of her scent. She smelled of wind, rain, and wildflowers. He'd noticed that about her the previous night, her sweet natural perfume. When they'd struggled together, her scent had marked him somehow, and all through the night he'd smelled her on his hands, his clothing, everywhere. He'd been unable to breathe without thinking of her.

He'd masturbated with the vision of her in his mind, and the scent of her in his nostrils. It had been so explosive a release for him that he'd wondered just how amazing the real thing would be. He'd grown so hot over the thought that he'd had to masturbate yet again before he could seek his rest.

He felt himself grow hard against her. Harder, he was forced to admit. Because ever since he'd first caught sight of her this night, brandishing her gun like a warrior princess, he'd had a raging hard-on for her. He felt her stir against him with her body's instinctive response to the dominating mastery of his. It made his cock thicken and grow longer against her, just that small shifting of her form against him.

He wanted her. He would not rest until he had her.

Admitting this truth to himself had become far easier than he'd thought possible in the past half-hour. He'd been fighting against the realization of the true depths of his attraction since he'd first seen her the night before. Now he wondered why he'd even bothered, for his surrender to the truth was far sweeter than any victory he'd ever known. His gaze roved down to the soft bow of her mouth and he was lost.

Cady had the space of a heartbeat to prepare herself, before he dipped his head down and tasted her lips. At that small, testing caress she felt a searing bolt of lightning rip through her. It was as if an electric current ran from his mouth to hers, making her see stars behind her fluttering lids. She moaned, surrendering and returning his kiss. She lifted her head to his and moved her lips fervently against him. It was the most stirring kiss she'd ever received in her life.

He parted her lips with a growl of male satisfaction, and speared his tongue deeply into her mouth. She met it with her own, eagerly. He tasted wild and untamed. Like pure, raging testosterone unleashed. Their teeth met as the kiss grew more heated, their lips meshed and their tongues thrust in a duel as old as time.

A wicked thrill danced through her when he drew her lower lip into his mouth. He suckled it as if it were a ripe fruit, lightly bringing his teeth to bear on the sensitive flesh. She moaned and squirmed against him. He was hard and hot against her. It was all she could do to keep from throwing her legs about his waist to rub against him until she came.

Oh hell, why not? Her legs came up and wrapped around him. He growled his response into her mouth, kissing her even more deeply.

It became difficult for Cady to catch a breath. Blackness swam inside her head and she tried to pull away, to breathe, but he would have none of it. He growled again and renewed his attack on her senses with an even fiercer kiss. She struggled—weakly because she was still caught up in the passion—but if she didn't breathe soon, she knew she was going to pass out.

Just when she thought she would lose consciousness, Obsidian puffed his own warm breath into her lungs and she was revived. His breath became her breath, and she depended upon him for each new burst of oxygen during their kiss. She knew she was making little mewling noises of excitement, but she didn't care. It was the most erotic experience of her life.

Cady tried to free her wrists from his imprisoning hand, but he was far too strong. He wouldn't let her budge, nor would he willingly set her free. She tried again, and this time he paused in their kiss to raise his lips from hers and look deeply into her eyes. She almost screamed at him for interrupting their kiss, until she was caught up in his burning gaze.

Their eyes were locked in silent combat—his seeking her surrender, hers seeking freedom. He moved against her, grinding his hardened cock more tightly against her already drenched and pulsing core. The feeling of his hard flesh against her was so arousing that she ceased struggling beneath him. He moved against her again, an undulating, rocking motion, and she eagerly tightened her legs and moved back against him.

He stilled. He looked from her gaze to her still imprisoned hands, and then back. He seemed to be waiting for something, some sign from her that she would no longer fight him should he choose to release her.

"Please...." she begged while shamelessly arching up against him, in search of more of that delicious friction he'd been so generous in giving her but moments before.

He seemed pleased with her response, and slowly released her hands, his movements clearly proving to her that he could recapture her at any time should he choose to do so. Her arms came around his shoulders, and she almost swooned to find how muscular and strong he felt beneath her hands. He was pure, masculine perfection.

Obsidian swooped down to resume their kiss, this one even more abandoned and passionate than the one before. Cady's hands roved all over his body — what parts she could reach — and Obsidian's did the same to her. His tongue speared deeply into the recesses of her mouth, and his hips moved and bumped his erection against her pelvic bone. One of his hands speared itself in her hair, while the other moved to cup a full breast, kneading her in such a way that it drove her crazy with lust.

Cady moaned and bowed her back, thrusting her breast more firmly into his hand. It felt burning hot against her, even through her clothing, as he squeezed her flesh. Strong fingers moved to pluck her nipple through the fabric of her shirt, and she felt it plump and harden, so tight she thought it would burst.

His gloriously skilled fingers pinched, pulled and twisted her nipple. His mouth moved from hers to trail a hot path down her jaw to her neck where he rooted and suckled and laved. She keened, a high, helpless sound of mindless excitement. The hand in her hair clenched, and she found herself wishing her hair was unbound from its braid so that he could clutch fistfuls of it the way she knew they both wanted him to.

Strong white teeth bit into the tender flesh of her neck, and she went wild beneath him. Her hands sought out his flesh under his garments and she sank her nails into him like a she-cat when she at last found it. She clenched her legs tight around him, dry humping him like a bitch in heat. Her mouth roved over his jaw, his ear, his neck, leaving hot, fierce kisses in its wake.

In the back of her mind she knew she should slow down in her wild flight towards ecstasy. After all, she didn't know this man, didn't know if she should trust him or fight him to the death. But the thought was swept away in the tumultuous storm of her arousal. Right or wrong, good or bad, she knew she hadn't a chance in hell of denying him. He played her body like an instrument, his masterful touch making her body sing beneath him.

She'd never been so ready for fucking.

Their clothes were an impediment to their progress. Obsidian rose up from her and brought both of his hands to the neckline of her shirt. Less than a second later he ripped it away from her with impatient strength, rending it cleanly down the middle. Her bra soon followed, the sound of tearing silk reminding her of the sound of tearing flesh.

Tearing flesh, gleaming fangs, snapping jaws. A feeling of dread and dark foreboding swept over her. Her body's arousal cooled, as quickly as if someone had dumped buckets of ice water over her flesh. A thrumming, electric hum suffused her whole body, but it was different from the wonderful feelings Obsidian had aroused within her. Far different.

A Daemon was near...maybe more than one.

"S-stop," she whispered. Her brain was scrambled, but her internal warning system was sounding a fierce alarm—bringing her back to the present, if only a little bit.

"Stop." Her command was a little surer this time. Not much, but a little.

Obsidian stilled with his hands resting on the fastening of her slacks. His gaze rose to meet hers, his expression inscrutable — guarded.

"You want me."

"Yes, I know, but it's dark out...it's night...*and something's wrong.*"

Immediately Obsidian was all business. In that moment, Cady could clearly see that he was indeed the fierce warrior he'd professed himself to be. That, and so much more.

"What is it?" He rose and helped her to stand.

"I can feel them." She closed her eyes and concentrated. It was difficult, but she forced herself to ignore the last lingering thrum his kisses had awakened within her. She opened herself to *other* things. "I can feel them moving."

"Where are they?" He clearly knew what she meant.

"Not far. Maybe a couple of miles."

"More than one, then?"

"I think so." She opened her eyes and met his gaze with her own.

"Get dressed," he commanded.

She gritted her teeth at his domineering tone. But she obeyed, since it was obvious that she couldn't fight the monsters naked. Even though the arrogant jerk would probably get a real kick out of *that*, she thought churlishly.

Chapter Six

"Wait here, human. I must go and gather my warriors. I'm now close enough to feel the threat and there are many of the Daemons. We should not try to take them alone."

"My name is Cady. *Kay-dee*. Use it."

"Wait here. I mean it. I will not tolerate any foolishness from you."

"You're not my keeper," she hissed.

They faced off in the darkness of the woods. Though Obsidian seemed to have the uncanny ability to cloak himself in the darkest of shadows, Cady could still see his jaw clench in frustration.

"We don't have the time to argue, Cady. I would take you with me when I go to gather my crew, but I do not know where I might find them. They might be patrolling the Gates, a place where no human can go. You would die if I took you there, for the place is hostile to humans, close as it is to the world of the Horde."

"You could try asking, instead of bossing me around. I'm not one of your warriors."

"No, but if we are to join forces, you will likely fall under my command. Get used to it now, for your own safety."

"I never said I would join you."

"Just stay here," he bit out.

"Fine!" They were standing toe to toe, neither ready to back down completely.

Obsidian seemed to relax a little after a moment. "I'll be back in a moment. Be silent. Be alert."

"Well, *duh*."

He sent her a strange look, and she had to remind herself that he wasn't human. He probably wasn't hip to much of her slang. The thought brought a sudden grin to her lips, displaying both of her dimples. She looked forward to flooding her language with similar words he wouldn't understand. She could tell it would really annoy him after a while.

A girl had to have her goals, after all.

"Sure, I'll chill out here. No problemo. I'm cool. Catch ya' later, 'kay?"

With a frustrated growl, and one last stern glare, Obsidian vanished before her eyes.

"Wow. Now *that* was cool," she whispered to herself. Soon her grin faded from her lips and she squared her shoulders. "Now to get down to business." With those words she popped a new clip into her mini-Uzi and moved silently into the shadows.

* * * * *

"What the Horde is that woman doing?"

"She looks like she's...taking a walk."

"Through a wood? At night? With no man to protect her, she'd have to be out of her mind."

"Cinder, I think it's safe to assume that she is out of her mind. Most humans, slow witted though they are, know better than to walk around a darkened wood at night. I *think*."

"But, Edge, how will we keep her safe from the Daemons without alerting her to their presence? Or ours? The creatures are too close to hope they haven't scented her. She's giving off plenty of psychic emanations. You know how they have a ravenous hunger for the psychically gifted. How can we protect her?"

"I have no idea."

"Edge, Cinder, on your guard."

The two men whirled around at the command. "Bloody Horde, Obsidian. Where have you been?" Edge asked.

"Seeing to business. Which is what you should be doing as well. I thought you were on patrol tonight. What's brought you out here?"

"The Elder relieved us of Gate duties tonight," Edge told him. "He told us to patrol this Territory instead."

"He told us it could be a learning experience for all of us," added Cinder. "A statement that I'm inclined to agree with. I've already learned that mortals are a very strange bunch. Take the woman in that grove of pines for example. She's just strolling through the trees with no thought to her own safety. It's most peculiar."

Obsidian came beside his men and looked through the foliage that concealed them. "What woman?" he growled. He suddenly had a strange feeling that he knew just who the woman in question was.

"That one there." Edge pointed through the trees. "The only one around for leagues."

Obsidian looked, his face filled with dread and exasperation, and swore. "Shit. I told her to stay put. *She's almost half a league away from where I left her.*"

"You know her?" asked Cinder, his tone puzzled.

"Who is she?" interjected Edge.

"That, my friends, is the legendary Cady—scourge of the Horde, protector of the Territories, and the most stubborn woman I've ever had the misfortune to meet."

"Amazing," breathed Edge in awe.

"That's Cady? But she looks so...*harmless*."

"Her appearance is deceptive; I've the bruises to prove it. I was sent here to speak with her the last two nights—that's why I haven't been on patrol with you. The Elder wants her to join our ranks. Though she's proving most difficult to recruit."

"A mortal...one of us? But why? Granted, she may be the fiercest warrior outside of our own kind, but she cannot help us patrol the Gates. No mortal can." Cinder sliced his hand through the air decisively, leaving tendrils of fire dancing through the air. He was after all an Incinerator, and those of his Caste were flame handlers.

"I trust The Elder knows what he is about. It is not for us to question his motives." Obsidian stoically refused to dwell on the fact that he had already done so, though it hadn't gained him any answers from Tryton.

"So that's the legendary Cady, hmmm? That would explain why she's giving off such strong psychic emanations. I've heard rumors about her, about how similar her talents are to ours. I wonder just how gifted she is?" Edge trailed off and looked at Cady thoughtfully. "I've never actually met a psychic human before."

"Curb your interest, Edge. She may be a fierce warrior, but she's got the disposition of a Horde Canker-Worm. Where is the Traveler?"

"I am here," spoke a dark voice from deep within the shadows.

"Show yourself," Obsidian commanded.

A tall, cloaked man emerged from the shadows. He moved silently, fluidly. "Have you need of my services, Obsidian?"

"I have Traveled as much as I can tonight. I've already drained much of my strength by doing so, looking for all of you. I'll need you close by during this battle. I won't have the strength to take us home should we have need."

"It shall be as you command."

The man stepped silently back into the shadows. Even with their exceptional night vision, which allowed them to see as clearly as a human would by daylight, there was no sign of where The Traveler lay hidden.

Obsidian turned back to Edge and Cinder. "Now wait here while I go and—" There was a sudden explosion of sound throughout the woods.

The Daemons had arrived. And they were hungry.

Before the three men could make a move, a Daemon came into view. One huge leap and the monster was flying through the air—straight at Cady. Obsidian made to shout a warning to her, but even before the words had left his panic-choked throat, she moved to strike at the monster.

She lunged upward, meeting the Daemon in mid-air. One hand deflected a blow from the monster. The other hand aimed the mini-Uzi at the beast's chest. A spurt of ammo and they both fell to the ground, with Cady standing over the fallen Daemon.

The fight had lasted mere seconds.

"*By Grimm's name,*" all three men swore in unison.

There was no more time for gawking, as heartbeats later four more Daemons moved into the thicket. Even as Cady set fire to the fallen form of her adversary, Obsidian, Edge and Cinder moved to engage in their own battles. The night's work was begun.

* * * * *

Cady looked about her. She'd only killed three beasts thus far, and already her clothes were caked with Daemon blood. She looked around her and saw Obsidian, and two men who she assumed were members of his fighting crew. She was relieved to see that she wasn't the only one who couldn't seem to keep from getting filthy during a Daemon fight. They all looked to be just as dirty as she was.

She walked toward them, ignoring the sickening smell of burning Daemon flesh that surrounded her. She was used to it by now. Well sort of, anyway.

"How many does that make tonight, Sid?" she asked.

"Excuse me? What did you call me?" Obsidian asked incredulously.

"Sid. It takes too much time to say Obsidian all the time—no offense."

"Well I do take offense. My name is an honorable one, given to me for—"

"Just answer the question. I'm too tired to argue with you right now."

Obsidian gritted his teeth. "I've killed four. Cinder, Edge—how many have you taken?"

"Two."

"Two for me as well."

"So with my three that makes eleven. My God, their numbers are rising every night. My record is only eight kills in a night, and a few years ago I would have thought five was the most I'd ever see at once." She glanced at her watch; the face was covered in Daemon blood but luckily it was waterproof, and when she wiped it clean she could see it was still functioning properly. "It's only three a.m., the night is still young. There could be more."

"I had no idea so many were escaping our patrols at the Gate. This is madness," one of the men said.

"Cady Swann, allow me to introduce you to two of my warriors. This is Cinder. He's of the Incinerator Caste. One of the best."

A man with whitish blond hair, standing at about six-foot-five, bowed low at the waist to her.

"It is an honor to meet you, Cady."

"Likewise. What does it mean—Incinerator Caste?"

"It is my class distinction within the Shikar society. The family to which I belong. Though, like any warrior I am skilled in many fighting arts, my greatest skills lie with the ability to make fire. When my team fells a Daemon I incinerate the remains while they move onward down the battlefield. I keep the fallen Horde from rising again." So saying he demonstrated for her.

Cinder held a hand out towards one of the already burning Daemons, and a ball of fire shot out to send the burning carcass exploding into even more flame.

Cady tried not to look uncomfortable. What Cinder was doing was oddly familiar. She looked away from the fiery display.

Obsidian drew her attention again. "This is Edge. He is of the Foil Master Caste."

A man with dark auburn hair, standing just an inch shorter than Obsidian, stepped forward. He also bowed and greeted her. Even before Cady had a chance to ask him about his Caste, he showed her exactly what it meant.

Twirling like a dancer, moving far more swiftly than her eyes could follow, the man raised his arms and sent blue-white blades shooting from his arms in all directions. The blades were the same as the ones she'd seen Obsidian use against her the night before. Only these flew through the air like boomerangs, glowing brightly in the night as they soared around in all directions before flying back into Edge's arms.

"*Holy moly.* So those things are called foils? Do all Shikars have them?"

"Yes, but only those of the Foil Master Caste can use them as projectile weapons," answered Edge.

"Amazing. Are these all of the men in your group, Sid?

Obsidian ignored her use of a nickname instead of his full name this time. He suspected she did it on purpose to get a rise out of him, and he'd be damned before he gave her the reaction she wanted. "There's just one more in my crew, for now. Traveler!" he called out.

In the blink of an eye a man appeared at Cady's side. She was so startled that she jumped back and raised her gun before she realized he wasn't making any threatening moves. She lowered her gun slowly and eyed the newcomer cautiously.

"The Traveler is new to my crew, though he was the personal Traveler of The Elder until Tryton assigned him to us."

"Tryton. That's the guy who wants me to join up with you guys, right?" she asked, remembering the short back-story Obsidian had supplied her with as they'd made the trek out into the woods earlier in the night.

"Yes, he's the one. He is our wisest and oldest leader. He felt that this Traveler was the best, and thus he assigned him to aid my crew."

"And I take it your crew is the best?" Her tone was droll.

"Of all the warriors in all the armies of the Shikar, my men are the most skilled, the most brave, and the most respected of any."

"Very nice. So, is Traveler your name or your Caste or what?" Cady asked, turning to the man who had as yet remained still and silent. His face and form were hidden beneath a heavy black cowl, but he stood tall and lean beside her. He was at least seven feet tall if he was an inch. She had to crane her neck up to look where his eyes should be beneath the hood.

"My name is unimportant." His voice was deep and smooth. "I am The Traveler, my Caste is Traveler, and my abilities are self-explanatory."

"Okay. Excuse me for asking. *Sheesh.*"

"How often do you find Daemons in this Territory?" asked Cinder, drawing her attention away from the hooded Traveler.

"Well it used to be about once every week or so. Sometimes a month would go by and there would be nothing. In the past three months, though, I've met up with them almost on a nightly basis."

"Then they are gaining in strength…or our patrols are failing," Cinder said.

"What patrols? Do you know why these creatures are suddenly running loose all over my town?"

The three men whose eyes she could see exchanged weighted glances. Cady assumed that Traveler shared in whatever unspoken communication passed between the other men. She really hated being ignored.

"Well, since you guys seem to have some dialogue to share without little ol' me interrupting, I'll just be going—"

"No. You will come with us and meet The Elder."

"What if I don't want to meet him? Maybe I have other appointments to keep tonight."

After hearing her words, Edge moved to speak. "By that you mean you will hunt for more Daemons? Surely you do not think there will be more of these creatures to hunt tonight?"

"No, there aren't any more out tonight. I just have other—"

"How can you be sure?" Edge asked, interrupting her.

With a weighty sigh, Cady closed her eyes and sent her senses seeking out into the night for signs of any more Daemons. All she felt was the still, calm quiet of the night around her. A moment later she opened her eyes and leveled her gaze at the men who flanked her. "I don't feel any. If there were more I would feel them."

"You can sense them? *Track them*?" Cinder turned to Obsidian. "But I thought she—" Obsidian silenced Cinder with a hard stare. Whatever Cinder had meant to say, Cady could see it was obvious that Obsidian didn't want him to finish.

"Look, guys, this is starting to grate on my nerves. If you can't speak openly in front of me, why should I bother cooperating by going to meet this Elder of yours? How do I know he'll be any more forthcoming with me than you have been?"

"We are being guarded from sharing information with you, because it is not our place to tell you Shikar secrets. The Elder will explain all you need to know. Aren't you a little curious about why you have been chosen to lead the life you do?" Obsidian asked.

"You mean in a cosmic sense? I always figured it was just bad luck."

"It would only be bad luck if you lacked the skills necessary to meet these monsters in battle. Gifted as you are — psychically and physically — haven't you ever wondered how or why you've been so well equipped for fighting The Horde?"

"Sometimes," she admitted.

"Then come with us. Meet The Elder. And wonder no more."

"How do I know I'll be safe? How can I trust you? I don't know you — and so far all you've done is attack me in my home, and bully me into following your orders."

"You attacked her?" Edge asked, shock in his voice.

Obsidian ignored him. "I give you my word that no harm will befall you when you go to meet Tryton."

"But not during or after my meeting? *No.* Forget it," she sighed, weary all of a sudden. "I can take care of myself, if it becomes necessary. Let's go see Tryton."

"Traveler, take us home," Obsidian commanded.

Everyone but Cady stepped forward at once to lay a hand upon The Traveler's now outstretched arm. Cady watched the men for a few heartbeats, unmoving, until she felt the heavy weight of The Traveler's gaze as he turned his head towards her.

"You must touch me if you wish to come with us." His voice was dark and smooth, like a moonless night.

Cady stepped forward cautiously, and laid her hand upon his. A vibrant jolt of electricity seemed to race from his flesh to hers, and for a single heartbeat she thought she could see his eyes beneath the deep cowl he wore. They were the color of darkest, blackest night—like windows to an infinite nothing.

With a gasp she looked away and met Obsidian's golden gaze. For a moment she felt safer, until his gaze heated and she remembered how they'd begun the night—in each other's arms. Before she could think on it further, however, the ground fell out from beneath her feet.

Seconds later she looked around, only to find herself standing within a great stone chamber unlike any she'd ever seen before.

Chapter Seven

"Welcome, little warrior, to our humble home," came a deep voice from behind her.

Cady turned toward the voice and beheld the sight of a man with platinum-blond hair, dressed entirely in black. Standing before an immense fireplace, he was tall and proud in bearing, with broad shoulders and thick muscles. His face had an untamed, leonine quality, and his eyes were bright yellow.

He was obviously another Shikar.

"Where are we?" she asked. Though the question was aimed at no one in particular, she felt curiously deferent to the yellow-haired man before her and looked to him when she spoke.

"You are far beneath the Earth's crust, though if humans were to dig to find us they could not. This place lies in a realm between worlds, safe from any harm that might be visited upon it otherwise."

"Like another dimension?"

"Precisely." The man eyed her closely, as if she were a puzzle he wanted to solve. "So you are the mortal warrior we've heard so much about. You must have many questions that warrant answers—but for now Obsidian will show you to the rooms we have prepared for you."

"Whoa, whoa, whoa—wait a minute! I don't need any rooms prepared, I just want to see this Elder guy and clear a few things up. Right here, right now."

"But surely you must feel ill-dressed for the occasion," the man said, gesturing to her filthy clothes. "A bath and some fresh attire will see you more prepared for your meeting."

She *did* feel scruffy, and meeting the obviously important Tryton in her present condition might put her at a disadvantage. "All right," she conceded and turned to look at Obsidian, who seemed far too interested in the exchange. "Lead on, Sid."

The blond man coughed. Cady would have sworn it was to cover up a bark of laughter. Obsidian's eyes heated angrily at her continued use of the nickname, and she tried valiantly not to smile at him in devilish glee. He was proving to be so much fun to torment.

"Follow me," he growled.

* * * * *

When Obsidian and Cady had departed from the chamber, Tryton turned to dismiss Edge and Cinder, but motioned for The Traveler to stay behind.

"I assume you witnessed the night's battles, my friend. What do you think of her?"

"She is far more talented than we had guessed."

"Did she display much of her psychic gifts during the battle?"

"It's difficult to say. She's faster and stronger than most mortals I've encountered. This was more than evident. But as for the other...I saw none of it tonight, but that does not mean the skills are not there."

"Perhaps she just needs training to learn the use of it?"

"Perhaps. There is, however, an unexpected development." The Traveler turned and removed the cowl from his head. His dark hair gleamed with blood-red highlights in the firelight. "She is a Hunter."

"She can track the Daemons psychically?" Tryton's voice was surprised, and thoughtful.

"As well as any Shikar of the Hunter Caste."

"This was unforeseen. Indeed she is gifted, to possess so many Shikar qualities. We must convince her to join with us. We have much to learn, each from the other."

The two men stared long into the flames, each consumed with his own thoughts concerning the human woman Cady Swann. And her future role within their army.

* * * * *

Cady looked down at the massive sunken tub with a wry grin. If the Shikars took baths in similar tubs every time they got into a skirmish with a Daemon, it stood to reason that their water bills were outrageous. She laughed at the thought of a Shikar warrior doing something so mundane as paying a utility bill. She doubted such a thing existed here in their world.

Obsidian had left her to her own devices after leading her to the rooms in which she now found herself. He'd escorted her through the vast, winding stone hallways in complete silence until they'd arrived at their destination.

"These are your apartments. I trust you will find everything in order within." After biting out those words, Obsidian had bowed slightly and made to leave.

"Wait. You can't just leave me here. How will I find my way around?" she'd asked.

"I will escort you to Tryton after we have both bathed and clothed ourselves. There is no need for you to wander about, and a good possibility that, should you do so, you will become quite lost. So I suggest you enjoy your bath and await me as patiently as you can."

"*Pendejo*...worthless jerk," she'd growled irritably as he'd left her standing there outside the door to her 'apartments.' Within she'd found an opulent three-chambered suite consisting of a large living room, bedroom and bathroom—complete with a sunken tub the size of a swimming pool.

Not knowing how much time she had to clean up she quickly undressed and slipped into the already filled bathtub. Finding a cake of floral scented soap and a washing cloth in a basket near the tub's rim, she lathered and scrubbed at the muck clinging to her body.

Wishing for some normal, everyday shampoo, and seeing none at hand, she resigned herself to using the cake of soap to cleanse her hair. When she felt confident that there were no stray pieces of Daemon gunk in her hair she rinsed and emerged from the filthy bathwater.

She found a neat stack of clean towels near what she assumed was a commode, though it was a little different looking from the ones she was accustomed to. It was only after she'd dried and wrapped her body within a towel that she realized she had no clean clothing to change into. Her earlier attire was hopelessly ruined. No amount of scrubbing would make them presentable, and even if she could hand wash them in the tub they wouldn't be dry before Obsidian came to retrieve her.

Just as she thought of Obsidian she heard a knock at the door. Tightly securing the towel around her body, she opened the door a crack.

"Are you done with your bath? I've brought you clean clothing," Obsidian said, nudging her aside and entering the room as though he owned the place. He looked as though he'd come straight from his own bath to meet her. His hair was damp, and unbound it fell to his waist.

He looked delicious.

"Come on in, Sid. Make yourself at home," she muttered.

"Sarcasm ill becomes you, Cady—" the rest of his words cut off abruptly as he got his first good look at her. His eyes immediately heated and roved over the exposed flesh of her shoulders and legs.

Cady strived not to feel completely nude before his hungry gaze, but the way he was looking at her, as if he would gobble her up in one gulp, was making it difficult to act unaffected.

"Your skin looks like melted caramels," he said in the sexiest, most masculine voice she'd ever heard.

"Well you can thank my father. I get my coloring from him." She laughed softly. "Do you even know what a caramel is?" she asked, trying to lighten the situation a little. She felt like she was swimming in waters too deep for her to tread.

"Of course. They're the sweetest, stickiest candies I've ever tasted. I can't help but wonder...will you taste as sweet? Will you grow as sticky if I warm you with my hands...my mouth?"

Her heart thudded, but he didn't give her a chance to reply. Instead he moved forward—faster than she could see—and swept her up into his arms. He slammed his mouth down on hers, wrapping her up in a passionate kiss, as he strode towards the bedroom. Cady couldn't think, could only feel his mouth on hers, and then she was flying through the air.

She landed softly on the bed, a huge canopied bed with deeply piled pillows and covers. Obsidian came down upon her, divesting her of the towel—her only covering—with a tug. His eyes devoured her exposed form, lingering on her full breasts and hips.

"Who would have thought such a lush bounty was hidden under your clothes," he breathed in pleased wonder.

"I always wear a good sports bra. It wouldn't do to have my breasts swinging about during a fight, you know." She averted her eyes. "And my hips have been wide since puberty—no matter how much I exercise I can't slim them down," she whispered, uncomfortable under his intense stare.

"It is a crime that such magnificent breasts be bound, and your hips," his hands gripped the body part under discussion, "your hips are just fleshy enough for a man to grab hold of when he rides you. Men like a little meat on their women, and I'm certainly no exception."

"I'm by no means a svelte *Seventeen* model. I'm just boring ol' me." Had she ever cared before this moment? Not that she could remember, but there it was—she was uncertain. She wanted him to like her despite what society would see as her physical flaws.

"You are so beautiful it hurts my eyes to look upon you," he said, and though his words were meant to be light he couldn't keep his voice from turning dark and passionate.

"That was the most perfect thing to say," was all she could manage.

"You shave your mons," he said, his eyes burning her there.

"My *mons*?" She laughed at the word. "Yeah, I do. Is that a problem?"

"No, I love it," he vowed, still staring in fascination.

With those last words he swooped down and sucked a plump nipple into his mouth, sending her senses reeling. His hair fell about them, caressing her like thousands of tiny fingers, cool against her heated skin.

His mouth fed at her, making slurping noises against her breast. He nipped and tongued, licked and pulled until she felt swollen and feverish. He laved his tongue in a hot, wet trail down the crevice between her breasts, moving his hands up from her hips to squeeze and knead them. His head moved downward, his lips nipping at her stomach, his tongue delving into her navel.

He breathed hotly over her hips before he brought his teeth to bear against her hipbone. With an impatient growl he brought his hands down to spread her legs, fingers digging into the flesh of her inner thighs to hold them apart. Cady gasped as she felt his hot, velvety tongue flick out to taste her exposed center.

He licked her pussy lips, suckling and nibbling at the folds of her labia. He buried his face against her and breathed deeply of her scent. Intoxicated with her, he speared his tongue into her slit, gathering as much of her fluids as he could before drinking them down.

He came up long enough to mutter darkly, "You taste far sweeter than caramel," before he dived for her flesh once more.

She cradled his head to her sopping wet core, fingers buried in his dark hair. Her body arched uncontrollably against his mouth, and she groaned like an animal. His tongue now moved in long, firm strokes against her clit, making it swell and pulse. She gasped and writhed as he licked her, and her orgasm took her in a rush, wracking her body with exquisite release.

Her body trembled as she came down from her climax, and she felt Obsidian give her one last, lingering lick. He suckled her clit as if in reward for her response to his attentions, and released it with a loud popping sound. Two long, strong fingers slipped inside of her, testing and stretching her.

"You're so tight. So hot and wet. I can't wait one more second," he growled.

"Don't wait," she begged shamelessly. "I want you to fuck me so hard we're both bruised by it," and she meant every word too. She'd never been so aroused in her entire life, and even though she didn't really know this man, she wanted him to pound into her until it didn't matter anymore. If there were to be regrets she'd have them later. For now she would indulge in the best sex of her life.

Her words seemed to drive him crazy, and her body writhed in response when he pulled back from her and began to remove his clothes. Within heartbeats he was as naked as she and it afforded her the first glimpse of his magnificent body.

He was fashioned like a god.

Obsidian raised himself up above her and positioned the great purple head of his cock against her wet slit. But he didn't immediately enter her. Instead he took her lips in a hot, wet kiss. He brought his lips, teeth, and tongue to bear against her mouth and fed there as though he were starving for her. She tasted herself in the kiss and went wild, arching her cunt up against him, trying to force him to slip into her where she needed him most.

His mouth smiled against hers, and he was pleased that she was so responsive to him. She felt like silk and fire in his arms, and where his cock rested against her he could feel the wet heat of her arousal. She let out a growl like some wild animal and moved her hands down to tug his hips closer to hers.

"Are you ready then?" he asked with a chuckle, knowing full well that she was.

"Yes. *Now*," she demanded.

"As you wish," he said and thrust to the hilt, his balls coming to rest against her buttocks.

Cady's breath left her on a gasp. She felt stretched, full to bursting. Her flesh burned where he filled her, and his cock reached deeper into her than she ever would have thought possible. It felt like she'd been spitted on a tree trunk. It was wonderful.

Obsidian's vision was hazy in his passion. He'd never been inside a woman who was as tight or hot as Cady. Never wanted one with such an all-consuming urge to conquer and possess. Her pussy walls pulsed and gripped the thick flesh of his cock, fitting around him as if she were made just for him. Only for him. He wanted her to feel just as affected by their joining as he was, and vowed to give her the ride of her life.

Bracing his hands on either side of her head he started to move within her. Slowly at first, then increasing the pace. His hips pistoned against her, and the force shook the frame of the bed beneath them. Struggling not to lose control as he approached one of the greatest orgasms of his life, he went a little wild and thrust into her wet heat with a jarring force.

"Did I hurt you, baby?" He paused, not wanting to harm her further if it were so.

Cady had never been so aroused, so sexually charged. She loved the power of his thrusts, and the barely contained violence behind them. In answer to his question she gave a feral grin, and rose up to sink her teeth into the strong muscle of his shoulder. He roared his response and pummeled her with his body.

Their bodies made wet, slapping sounds, but the noises only spurred them on. Cady raked her nails down his back, then kneaded the firm, flexing muscles of his buttocks as he pounded into her. Obsidian brought her ankles up and over his shoulders. She felt his cock pulse deep inside of her, and came on a scream.

Obsidian groaned at the exquisite feel of her honeyed walls gripping at his dick. He thrust twice more, before pulling his cock free of her body and shooting his come onto the soft swell of her stomach. After he'd bathed her in his sperm he collapsed at her side, breathing harshly into her ear.

After a few moments Cady found her voice. "Why didn't you come inside of me? I'm on the pill, you don't have to worry about pregnancy."

After a weighty silence he answered, eyes averted, "I never spend myself in a human woman. It's not acceptable among my kind to spend our seed in such a way."

Cady tried not to feel stung by his words. She'd known not to expect anything from their joining. After all, they barely knew each other. But it still hurt to have the truth of it rubbed in her face.

"Well next time try to shoot your load somewhere besides all over your partner. It's no fun being creamed on and having to clean up afterwards, I can assure you."

"You needn't get offended. I'll be happy to bathe my seed from your skin." His eyes flashed hotly at the prospect. "I normally wear protection to avoid this type of situation…but I'm sure that neither of us were prepared for such an encounter tonight."

"I know, and you're right. I'll clean up and get dressed. I'm sure Tryton is wondering what's keeping us."

While Cady went to the bathroom Obsidian donned his own clothing, wondering how best to prepare her for the meeting with Tryton.

"The Elder probably already knows what's been keeping us."

"What do you mean?" she called out.

"He has ways of knowing things. Ways you or I will never understand. He's not called The Elder merely because of his age, but also because of his Shikar skills. He's earned much respect over the years, and is very wise. He'll know what we've been doing here, doubt it not."

"Well I don't care. What business is it of his anyway? Does he have a say about whom you have sex with?"

"I'm sure you know he does not. I would hope you at least knew enough about me now to guess I would never allow such a thing," he bit out.

"Well at least I don't have to worry that he commanded you to use yourself as bait to woo me into your little club." Dressed now in the loose cotton trousers and shirt that Obsidian had brought her, she came into the bedroom trying to detangle her hair.

"Do you have a brush or comb anywhere? My hair's a mess."

Crossing to a dresser he picked up a strangely shaped comb. The teeth were crooked and widely spaced, and the handle was broad and curved. She accepted it with a soft thank you.

Obsidian watched her brush her hair in silence, oddly seduced by the sure strokes of the comb through her dark mane. "There's so much of your hair. I never would have thought so, the way you braid it so tightly."

"I haven't ever cut it except to trim the ends. My Grandmother used to tell me it was my one true vanity. I think she was glad I had at least one." She smiled at the memory, preparing to secure her hair in its customary braid.

"You should leave it down. I like it swaying around your hips...I'd like to see it thusly when you're riding me." His voice had gone all sexy again, sending shivers down her spine.

"I don't think I want to have my first meeting with your Elder with my hair all over the place. I want to be comfortable and neat in front of him." She deliberately avoided responding to his sexual innuendo.

Her insides melted when she thought about riding him. She wondered if she'd ever let there be such an event between them. She'd enjoyed their sex. In fact she'd never had better. But Obsidian was dangerous. In her heart she knew that if she let him he'd invade her every waking thought. It would probably be wiser if she avoided any more encounters with him.

Turning to face him, her face serene but for a determined look in her eye, she said simply, "I'm ready to meet him now."

Chapter Eight

"You're Tryton?" Cady's words were more an accusation than a question.

"Yes. And you are Cady Swann." Tryton's full lips tugged against a smile. He turned to Obsidian who was standing at her side. "You may leave us, Obsidian. Cady and I have much to discuss."

For a moment Cady thought he would protest. But after a lengthy silence, and one quelling glance in her direction, Obsidian quit the room. Immediately she turned to face Tryton.

"I should have known it was you earlier tonight."

"Why is that?"

"Because Sid obeyed you when you told him to take me straight to my rooms. I doubt he obeys many people."

Tryton threw back his shining head and laughed. It was an honest and open laugh, but for some reason Cady didn't think he laughed very often. After a few more guffaws, he quieted down, but a smile still played about his mouth.

"You're right. Our friend Obsidian is more used to being obeyed by others. But he defers to me out of mutual respect. Not rank or obligation."

"I see what you're getting at. You don't force obedience. You earn it."

Tryton motioned for her to sit in an oversized chair near the fire. "You and Obsidian have grown somewhat close in the last forty-eight hours."

"Is that a note of sarcasm I hear in your voice?" She fought to keep her voice neutral.

"You must forgive me, but from the way Obsidian described your first meeting, I would never have expected this so soon."

"By *this* you mean…what exactly?"

"Why, your mating, what else? Did you think I would not know?" His voice was chiding but his eyes were twinkling.

"Mating? What an odd, archaic word for you to use. We had sex, and yes it was a sudden development but we're both adults and of a legal age. I don't see what it has to do with you."

"It has nothing to do with me, of course. But I am nosy in my old age—"

"Old age? You don't look a day over forty. Probably less actually, when you smile," she said, a little confused.

"I am older than you would think. I make it a point to keep my true age a secret. But I will tell you that when Christ walked the Earth I was already a man."

Cady sat, stunned. She couldn't find a reply that wouldn't make her sound like a witless idiot. He *was* old.

"As I was saying, I am nosy and I make it a point to know when a relationship springs up between one of my fiercest warriors and a human woman. It's not a common occurrence, I can assure you."

Brushing aside her amazement over his age, she suddenly scowled. "You know, I'm getting tired of hearing humans spoken of with the same distaste someone might show for a pile of dog shit. If your race is so advanced, so *superior* to mine, then why do you hide away from us? Why haven't I met any of you before?"

Her voice had risen over the last few words, and she paused to compose herself.

"You're angry. I meant no offense by my words, truly. I have respect for your race, despite their shortcomings. Were your rooms comfortable?" He changed the subject.

"You know they were. Why am I here?"

"You don't mince words. Very well then, neither will I. We want you to join us in the fight against the Horde."

"Why me? Don't you have enough recruits or whatever?

"Because you are a puzzle, young Cady. A surprise. You belie every preconception we've ever held about humankind and it has intrigued us. You have psychic gifts, a thing almost unheard of among your people. You're fearless and legendary in battle. For these reasons and more we want you to come and fight with us."

"But I've been doing this for fifteen years. Why contact me now?"

"Believe it or not, we had no knowledge of this threat in the Territories until just a few short years ago. Since then I've learned much about you. You're a very secretive woman. It was hard to learn any facts about you."

"At least I have *that* reassurance." Her voice fairly oozed sarcasm.

"Your parents died when you were fourteen. In a tornado?"

It was several moments before she answered. Tryton seemed content to wait her out. "No. But that's what everyone believes."

"They died in a Daemon attack?"

"If you already know the details why are you questioning me?" She was getting defensive. The memories were always painful, and Tryton seemed determined to dredge them up.

"I want to hear it from your own lips. I have my reports on the incident, but they might be incomplete. How did they die?"

"In an attack. Three of the monsters stormed into our house and killed my parents." Images flashed through her mind like snapshots from a crime scene. She tried to detach herself from the pain that always came when she spoke of her family.

"You had a little brother." It wasn't a question. Tryton already knew the answer, having gained the information from his spies. But he wanted to hear it from her own lips.

"I don't want to talk about this."

"What happened to your little brother?" he pressed.

"I don't want to *fucking talk about this!*" she yelled. Her voice echoed off the great stone walls.

"You came downstairs when you sensed them. You saw them standing over the bodies of your parents, and you rushed them. They fled, taking your brother with them. He was still alive. You grabbed your father's gun and pursued them into the woods outside your home. I have this much information—but I need to hear all the details." His voice was hard as steel. "What happened to your brother?"

Several minutes passed.

"They took him." Her voice was thick with suppressed tears. "They took him outside, into the trees. It was windy—a storm was coming. I could smell the ozone in the air. I was scared of the storm, but I ran out after them with my Daddy's .22."

Silence. Then Tryton's voice urged her to continue. "What happened then?" he asked.

"I found them about a half-mile into the trees. The wind was roaring, but I could still hear them chewing…crunching away." She choked on a sob, and a solitary tear escaped to trail down her cheek. Tryton's heart wrenched in pity but he urged her to continue.

He needed to know if all he'd been told was true.

"They were eating my baby brother," she cried. "He was so small. He didn't have a chance in hell of fighting them off, and they killed him. Pulled him apart. Ate him all up…" she trailed off.

"What did you do?" Tryton was relentless.

"I was so mad I forgot to be scared. I fired the gun and caught one of the bastards in the back of the head. He fell over. The other two rushed me and I killed them too. I burned their bodies, and by that time the tornado had struck.

"It leveled my house and saved me the trouble of having to explain everyone's deaths to the police. Everyone assumed my parents were killed when the house caved in, and that my brother, Armand, had been carried away by the force of the storm. Armand was on a missing persons list for a little while, but a lot of people died in that storm. Everyone figured he had too."

"How did you kill the Daemons, Cady? A .22 rifle will not kill a Daemon. We both know this."

"I'm through talking to you." Her voice was pure ice.

"How?"

Long minutes passed. "I incinerated the motherfuckers. Just like Cinder does."

I knew it, Tryton thought. Aloud he said, "I'm sorry I had to make you relive those memories. You've never told anyone." It wasn't a question.

Cady answered anyway. "No. I let everyone think what they wanted. It was enough that I knew the truth."

"You went to live with your grandparents after that. Almost immediately you started hunting the Daemons, but your grandparents never suspected?"

"No. I snuck out of my window at night, when I knew a monster was near. If I got bruised up really bad or bloodied, I just let my grandparents think I was getting into fights after school. I didn't want to shock them with the truth. I learned by trial and error how best to kill the monsters, and as my skills improved I had fewer wounds to hide."

"Yet tonight, when you fought, my men didn't see you use your Incinerator abilities."

"I haven't been able to since that first time. I don't even know how it happened. One minute I was so mad I saw red—the next flames were shooting out of me. It was like I was a human torch or something."

"I'm not surprised. It takes a lot of power and control to summon fire. What about your other skills?"

Cady smiled and pushed away her pain with effort. "You mean my 'spooky talents?'" She laughed. "I can move faster and quieter than most people. I'm quite strong. I can see really well in the dark, and I can...*feel* when the Daemons are near."

"I was surprised to hear you have that ability. Few of our warriors have multiple Caste traits."

"How do you mean?" she couldn't help asking.

"You're obviously an Incinerator. And you can sense the Daemons. You can track them. These are traits of the Hunter Caste."

"But I'm a human, not a Shikar."

"Your psychic skills are what make you like us. Very few humans are gifted in such ways, but you are obviously one of them."

"What can I say? I'm a complex kinda girl," she quipped.

"I suspect this is why the Daemons fed on your brother. They thrive on victims with psychic gifts. I wager your sibling had his own Shikar abilities, and was therefore a lure to the beasts." Tryton fell silent, then met her eyes with his amber glowing ones. "I am sorry for your loss. More than I can say."

"Why do you need me?" she repeated her earlier question. "You've obviously got things covered here."

"The lands outside of the Gates—your lands—are called Territories. It's only been in recent years that Daemons have leaked out into your world. For eons we've been fighting them at the Gates between our three worlds, keeping them from escaping their boundaries."

"Well obviously somebody's sleeping on the job."

"But you see, they're not escaping through the Gates. They've found other ways out. That's why you've been seeing more and more of them. They are finding their way out through this...back door, so to speak."

"That still doesn't answer my question. Why would you want me to join your army? Don't you need me up there on Earth where I can fight these things?"

"You will still be up there. I am putting together a team of my best warriors. This team will be reassigned to patrol the Territories. We've never paid much attention to your lands before now, but I am seeking to rectify that. We need you on the team as an area expert."

"Ok. So if I volunteer, who else will be on the team?" She knew the answer before he gave it.

"Obsidian, Cinder, Edge, and the Traveler." Tryton smiled when she slumped in her seat. She looked more than a little disappointed in her prospective teammates. He wondered if Obsidian knew what he was getting into with this feisty human. It would be fun to watch the prideful warrior find out.

"I take it Sid will be the leader, or whatever," she bit out.

"Yes. He's an able warrior. One of my best. He's an excellent leader—born and bred for the duty."

"And what's with this Traveler thing—is that *really* his name?"

"He keeps to himself. He'll give you his name when he is ready," Tryton said in way of an answer.

"Antisocial is he?"

"Sarcastic aren't you?" he shot back.

Cady couldn't help grinning. He was a sharp devil, this Tryton. "Where are your women?" she asked as the thought occurred. She hadn't seen hide nor hair of a female since entering this place.

"They reside in a different part of the city. Our unattached warriors live here, that's why you haven't seen any women so far."

"Your warriors are all men?"

"Yes."

"Why? Are women forbidden from fighting or something?" She started to feel insulted on their behalf.

"No, of course not. Before now we've never encountered a woman, human or Shikar, who had fighting skills. You are the first." He smiled again, seeing her agitation.

"Well *whoop-de-do* for me. If I agree to fight with you, what will change for me? I mean besides the whole working with a group thing."

"You'll live down here with us during the day. During the night you'll join your teammates and hunt the Territories."

"I have a job during the day."

"You'll have to leave that behind." His voice was firm.

"Well no dice then, Mr. Elder. I have to have a normal life, if only for a few hours each day. It's kept me going this long, I'm not about to give it up."

"Our people cannot tolerate the sunlight. We do not go into the Territories during the day."

Cady growled. "I am not a Shikar so that hardly matters, does it?"

They both fell into silence for several moments. Tryton's amber eyes regarded her thoughtfully. She couldn't help but wonder what secrets he was keeping from her. She'd have to be an idiot to think he was telling her everything.

She was definitely not an idiot.

"Very well, Cady. I concede to you in this matter. You may live your human life by day, but by night you are a member of the Shikar Alliance. You will be a Protectorate of the Territories. Until such a time as you decide to change your lifestyle, of course."

"Yeah," she scoffed. "That'll be the day."

Chapter Nine

"It's dawn on your world. I don't suppose you can stay here for the day?" Tryton asked.

"No, I've got to feed my cat and go to work. By noon," she added.

"Don't you need to sleep? To rest?"

"I'll sleep when I'm dead," she joked. "Really, I'll be fine. I don't need much sleep. I'll grab a couple hours' worth before work."

"Very well then. Some of us can tolerate the early morning sun. Obsidian is one, but I think he's far too tired to attempt Traveling again. He's only good for two or three trips per night. I'll send the Traveler to take you home." He walked to the mantle of the fireplace and reached his hand into a small cloth bag that rested there. When his hand withdrew there was glittery sand in his pinched fingers. He threw it into the fire. The flames grew brighter, and Tryton muttered words in a language Cady didn't understand.

A second later, the Traveler appeared at her elbow.

"*Whoa,*" she exclaimed and jumped from her chair. The suddenness of his arrival had surprised her—again. "Give me some warning next time, *jeez.*" Her heart thudded in her chest.

"Take my hand." His voice was as dark as before.

"I haven't gathered my guns or clothes or anything," she protested, looking to Tryton.

"I'll have Obsidian bring them to you tonight. He'll meet you at your house, promptly at sundown," Tryton said with a small smile.

Cady's gaze shot up to the hooded darkness of the Traveler's face. He looked like the Grim Reaper standing so still and tall. Except he was much more muscular than she imagined Death could ever be. He seemed really...dangerous.

"Take my hand," he commanded again, reaching out to her. Cady squared her shoulders and laid her hand in his much larger one. She closed her eyes.

And opened them in her living room.

"That wasn't as bad as the first time," she remarked.

"You'll get used to it," said her companion, who moved to stand behind her.

"I hope so. How do you do that?" She turned to face him.

He was gone.

"Goodbye to you too," she griped. She felt a soft nudge against her feet and looked down.

"Hey, Squaker," she crooned as she bent to stroke the black cat. He must have come in through the pet door she'd installed, so he wouldn't be cooped up all day. "I bet you're hungry, aren't ya, boy? Let's go grab a bite then hit the hay." She scooped him up, nuzzling his silky head with her chin.

Her weariness pulled at her like a ton of bricks. But her growling stomach couldn't wait until breakfast. With a heavy sigh she went to the kitchen to forage for food. She might be able to squeeze two hours of sleep in before work. If she was lucky.

She needed a vacation. Though she doubted the monsters would understand or comply with her request for the time off.

* * * * *

For the umpteenth time, Cady winced as the sore muscles of her legs protested from her exertions. All she was doing was shelving the newest shipment of books. Not a difficult physical task to be sure. But her muscles ached and pulled anyway.

Obviously Sid had ridden her harder than she'd thought.

She'd heard of people being boned so hard they couldn't walk the next day, but this was ridiculous. Her muscles didn't hurt this much after a busy night fighting Daemons. Okay, so that was an exaggeration. But she rarely exerted her inner thigh muscles when fighting and was unused to this type of strain.

Well it had been worth any minor discomfort, she reminded herself. He was the best sex she'd ever had. All day long she'd been wearing a stupid grin on her face. She couldn't stop thinking of how good he'd smelled, how firm he'd felt. How fully he had stretched her with his massive cock.

No doubt about it, Sid was positively *yummy*.

"There you go again, grinning like a loon." The voice made her jump. Too many people were sneaking up on her, she thought with an inward snarl.

Ashley Gailey, one of her co-workers, stood next to her. Three inches taller than Cady, with blonde hair and blue eyes, Ashley had been homecoming queen their senior year in high school. She was now happily married with three kids. "So who's the lucky guy?"

"What? There's no guy. What are you talking about?" Cady affected a mock look of surprise.

Ashley laughed at her antics, but there was no deterring her. "There's only two things that will put that smile on a woman's face. One's chocolate. The other's a man."

"Well, when you're right, you're right. It is a man." Cady faked a love-struck sigh. It wasn't too hard at all, surprisingly enough.

"Who is he?" Ashley squealed. "Is he from 'round town?"

"No."

"He's from the city then?"

"No."

Ashley's southern-belle good looks scrunched into a frown. "Well if he's not from 'round town, and he's not from the city then where is he from?"

"Another dimension." Cady laughed when Ashley gasped.

"Cady Swann, don't you go making fun of me! I was just curious is all." Cady kept laughing as Ashley continued, "Well I'm glad you've found a man that can put up with your sense of humor for more than five minutes at a stretch. He must have the patience of a saint."

"Oh Ashley, I'm sorry. Yes, I'm grinning about a man and no, he's not from around here. He lives...pretty far away."

"Long distance relationships are hard. How long have you been together?"

"We've known each other almost seventy-two hours," she admitted.

Cady didn't know if the look Ashley sent her was one of surprise or approval. "Girl, you move fast. Good luck."

"Thanks." Cady knew she'd need all the luck in the world.

* * * * *

It was approaching sundown. Cady was in the middle of changing. The blouse she was removing tangled up around her head as she tugged it off. She grunted in frustration and wriggled to remove the shirt.

Large, warm hands came around and cupped her breasts.

Cady shrieked and the shirt was whisked away by a laughing Obsidian. "You should pay more attention to your surroundings. I've been here several seconds and you never even sensed me."

"You jerk," she shot back. She was standing there, in her satin bra and panties, totally disheveled. Of course he looked as delicious as ever. "You could have cleared your throat or something."

"But this way of greeting was so much more pleasant." His voice had gone all sexy on her.

Her heart had sped up but she tried not to let it show. "You're early. Tryton said you'd be here at sundown. There's still about ten minutes of daylight left."

"I was hoping ten minutes would be enough for us. Though now I'm not sure."

"For wha—" she had just enough time to gasp before Obsidian's lips landed on hers. He was *such* a good kisser.

"What are you doing to me, woman?" he growled against her mouth. His tongue darted in to taste her. "I can't stop thinking about you…about this." His hand swept down into her panties and cupped her. "Oh, baby, you're already wet for me."

She'd been wet for him all day.

Obsidian crooked one vein-roped arm, and Cady immediately threw a leg over it. He raised his arm higher, spreading her legs to allow his other hand better access. Two long fingers parted her folds and thrust into her. She mewled and moved against his hand, sucking on his tongue as it delved into her mouth again.

Their breathing was harsh and loud in her bedroom. The hand between her leg thrust in and out of her, stretching her and preparing her for his penis. His fingers hooked inside of her and pressed on her G-spot, causing her muscles to lock down on him in her pleasure.

Obsidian groaned in response. He'd thought of nothing but her since he'd risen for the night. Dreams of her had haunted him in his sleep. All he could think about was having more of her.

The memories of her sexy little body were nothing compared to the reality. Her cunt was as wet and tight as he remembered. And those little sounds she made in the back of her throat made him just as crazy now as they had when he'd been buried inside of her the night before.

He couldn't get enough of her.

"I can't wait. I have to have you now." He tore at her panties and bra.

She loved that he was such a ravenous beast. "I can't wait either," she vowed. Her hands went to the fastening of his trousers. His heavy erection sprang free and filled her hand. She pumped him once, twice, as he divested her of her underwear. He felt like velvet on steel. He was so hot he almost burned her hand. Cloth tore and she was naked at last.

Obsidian didn't wait. He lifted her and thrust into her with one smooth move. She wrapped her legs around him and seated herself more tightly against him. He was so deep inside she thought he must feel her heart beating with the head of his cock.

Cady's breasts bobbled as he bounced her, rocking in and out of her. Her cunt made a wet slurping sound with every thrust. Obsidian raised her a little and took a nipple into his mouth. His teeth closed over her and she shrieked with delight.

He moved to the other nipple and did the same.

The contractions of her vaginal muscles clamped down on him like a vise. He couldn't help groaning over the exquisite sensation and thrust into her harder. Her breaths panted in his ear, and he sucked hard on her breast. He was a little crazed, but couldn't control himself. She was so fucking sexy.

He was going to come.

With thrilling speed he took them to the floor, but was careful to lay her gently on her back. He spread her legs wider and pumped into her with greater speed and strength. They were both covered in sweat, and the perfume of their sex was heavy in the air. Obsidian angled his body so he ground against her clit as he rode her.

Cady screamed and her climax was upon her. She saw stars behind her scrunched lids. Shuddering, she spread her legs impossibly wider to accept his pumping hips. Her ears rang with his shout of release as he jerked out of her and moved down, spilling his semen onto the floor.

It was several moments before her senses returned and she realized what he'd done. It was like being doused with cold water.

Cady had never cared before if a man came inside of her. To be honest she'd never let one do so; she'd always insisted they use condoms. But the fact that Obsidian would spend himself on the floor rather than inside of her body upset her. It hurt her to know he kept that bit of himself from her.

Silence stretched between them. Obsidian struggled to catch his breath, and Cady brooded. Her body still felt deliciously loved, but her mind and heart felt bruised.

"I'm sorry, baby," he said. "I forgot condoms again."

"Why won't you come in me?" Had she meant to ask outright like that? She refused to feel embarrassed about it now.

Obsidian sighed. "It's against our laws. Our sperm can't be released in a human woman. If I were to do so the crime would carry severe repercussions. I'm sorry I made a mess on your floor. I'll clean it up."

"Goddammit, Sid, I don't care about how big of a mess you make. Sex is always messy, but that's not the point. I feel like…I don't know, like you don't think very highly of me when you hold back. It's insulting."

Obsidian's eyes widened. He'd never thought she would feel that way. He was holding back to protect her, though he couldn't tell her that. There was nothing he wanted more than to fill her with his seed, to feel that moment of release while still buried in her body. But there were more important things than his ultimate satisfaction.

Like her life.

"Never think that, Cady. I don't hold back from you because I necessarily want to. We're a different species you and I. Doesn't that concern you enough to want to take certain precautions?"

"I told you that pregnancy isn't an issue. I'm on the pill."

"That has no bearing on this," he sighed. "It's against our laws, so I will not come inside of you. Let us leave it at that."

"Fine," she said and shoved him off of her.

"Don't let this small thing mar what we've shared," he called out as she marched to the bathroom.

Cady splashed water on her face, thinking. Was she making too big a deal of it? Tiny tremors still traveled through her body, aftershocks from her breathtaking climax. He'd been a beast, wild on her, but he'd still seen to her pleasure first. Obviously he cared enough to see that she enjoyed herself.

And boy did she ever enjoy herself.

When she emerged from the bathroom, Obsidian had already righted his clothing and cleaned up the floor. His amber eyes were hot as fire as they roved over her nudity. She smiled, showing off her dimples. Shameless, she put a little sway into her hips as she turned her back and walked to her closet.

"You're playing with fire," he growled in her ear. Cady jumped, bumping into him. He moved so fast. It was something she'd never get used to.

"Quit sneaking up on me. Let me get dressed."

"If I could have my way you would never wear clothes again. I would have you naked and spread on my bed all hours of the day and night." The words shivered down over her skin. Lips pressed a hot kiss to her shoulder.

Cady's legs went weak as he ran his hands down over her arms. How could she want him like this again, so soon after she'd been thoroughly sated? It wasn't as if she normally acted like such a sex-starved maniac. There was just something about him that made her forget how tender and well loved she'd felt but moments before. Something that made her want to throw him down on the ground and impale herself on him over and over.

"I want you again." His words echoed her thoughts. "A thousand times wouldn't be enough. You've bewitched me."

No more than he'd bewitched her.

He pulled away, reluctantly. She was so soft in his arms, so perfect. He wanted to bury himself in her. Lose himself inside of her forever. It was crazy, complete madness. Despite knowing that the other members of his team would be there any moment, he wanted to take her again.

Never in all his years had he been so close to losing control.

"Get dressed." His voice was heavy with his passion. Ragged. "The night is upon us. We'll come back to this later."

Cady shivered. She couldn't wait.

Chapter Ten

It was getting close to midnight. Cady stood amidst three Shikar warriors, searching for signs of any Daemons. So far tonight they hadn't encountered even one of the beasts. Cady, at least, was grateful. She needed a night off.

"I still don't sense any," she said. "Considering the hour, I don't think we have to worry about any tonight. The Daemons' activities usually peak around midnight, and wind down as dawn approaches. "

"The backdoor must be near here. The Daemon's wouldn't stray too far for fear of being caught in the light of dawn. By Grimm, surely they would stay as close to their escape route as possible," Cinder noted.

"By grim? What a strange thing to say."

"Not really," Cinder began, obviously warming up to a favored topic. "We swear by Grimm's name because he is a powerful ancestor. Grimm was once our greatest and most feared warrior. He once smote down an entire army of Daemons with but a wave of his hand."

"He once defeated a Horde Canker-Worm *unarmed* – one of the foulest creatures ever to haunt the Gates," Edge added.

"What happened to him?" Cady couldn't help asking.

"He disappeared one day after a great battle between the Horde and the Alliance. Some say he was mortally injured and being of the Traveler Caste went to die in the realm beyond as Travelers often do." Flames danced from Cinder's eyes as he recited the tale.

"Others say he went mad. Travelers walk between worlds, and it can affect their minds. With so many different alternate realities and so many different dimensions, Travelers are often unable to distinguish one from the other once they gain in years. Grimm was already several hundred years old when he disappeared—older than many Travelers ever grow to be. It would be no stretch of the imagination if he became lost between the worlds and never found his way back to us." Obsidian paused and looked around. Cady suddenly realized that the Traveler wasn't with them, and wondered if *he* would someday meet the same fate as poor Grimm.

"Let's cease this talk of legends and continue searching for the backdoor," Edge said.

"What would this doorway look like?" Cady asked.

"There's no telling. But we'll know it when we see it."

Out of nowhere, the Traveler appeared. *Speak of the devil.* Cady grinned.

The Traveler's voice was like black velvet from within the shadows of his cowl. "Obsidian. Tryton thinks that tonight would be a good time to show Cady around our city. Edge, Cinder and I will stay behind and look for the backdoor."

"Good suggestion," agreed Obsidian. He reached out and grabbed Cady's hand. Before she could form a protest, they were standing in the middle of what she assumed was his bedroom. It certainly wasn't hers.

"Hey! You didn't even ask me if I wanted to come here. What if I had wanted to go home early?"

"Trust me, you don't." His eyes danced wickedly.

"How do you know? I'm missing out on some much needed sleep, actually."

"What if I promised to make it worth your while?"

Cady's eyes flared. She tried and failed to hide her excitement. "Well okay, I guess. If you *promise*."

"Take off your clothes."

She was startled at the terseness of his command. But his eyes burned with suppressed heat, so she eased. Her lips curved. "You too."

Hurriedly, they both shucked their clothing. "Won't Tryton be mad at the delay?" she couldn't help asking.

"He's not really expecting us for a few hours yet, I assure you. But it wouldn't matter anyway. I'm having you at least once before we leave this room."

Wow. Excitement zinged through her body, and she tore off the remainder of her clothes. Naked, they faced each other. The light was an amber glow all around them. It played lovingly over his bulging muscles, creating shadows beneath his heavy chest and ab muscles.

His arms bulged with strength. Shoulders, broad and strong filled her vision. Beneath his heavy torso his waist tapered into lean hips before flaring again into muscular thighs. Obsidian's body could have easily passed for that of a body builder. Cady couldn't help but wonder what it would look like oiled down. Or how it would feel all slippery against hers.

It was crazy to lust after his body this way. She barely knew him, though being in mortal combat with him had drawn them closer than would normally be possible in so short a time. Later she would remember all the things she was growing to like about this stubborn man's personality. But just now she wanted…well, *sex*. Lots of sex.

Cady moved closer to him and dropped to her knees. He was so tall she had to strain upward to place her face level with his jutting erection. Licking her lips, she reached out to grasp him in her fist. He was thick. Too thick for her fingers to reach all the way around him.

The hard flesh in her hand was hot as flame. She pumped him, and watched as the swollen flesh pulsed in response. A thick blue vein ran down the length of him and her tongue darted out to trace it. Obsidian moaned and moved against her body, instinctively seeking entrance into her mouth.

Breathing deeply, she took in his masculine scent. Her gaze rose and locked with his, and she deliberately licked the crown of his cock so he could watch. She'd never felt more powerful than when his eyes flared and his knees swayed upon seeing her tongue laving him.

It was plain to see that he loved watching her. She let a clear drop of her saliva fall on him, and used her hands to rub it all around. He let out a groan, staring in fascination. Pouting her lips out she bestowed upon him a suckling kiss, before taking the large head into her mouth.

The taste was salty-sweet and she wanted more. Her mouth widened and took him deep, until he butted against the back of her throat. Knowing it would vibrate down the length of him she moaned as she sucked up and down his cock. He was so thick, she had trouble keeping her teeth off of him, but it was worth her aching jaw muscles to see to his pleasure. Her head bobbed up and down as she worked, and her hands came up to massage his testicles.

Obsidian trembled to feel her hot, wet mouth stroking his cock. In all his life he'd never had a more talented set of lips wrapped around him. It was all he could do to keep from falling in a heap on the floor. He looked down and saw her mouth full of him, lips stretching around his girth. It almost undid him.

"Stop, baby, wait." His hands stilled her motions, though he couldn't resist moving in her one last time. "I have other plans," he promised. He pulled out of her mouth, and with a popping sound her lips reluctantly set him free. "Wait here," he instructed.

Cady rose to her feet as Obsidian turned and left the room. She barely had time to turn toward the bed before he had returned. She could see he had a handful of condoms and smiled. "Are you planning a long night for us then?" she couldn't help teasing.

"The longest ever." He grinned back at her.

"*Gasp.* Shock. I didn't know you could smile without it looking mean," she laughed out.

His eyes twinkled and he put the condoms on a stone pedestal by the bed. "There's something I want you to do for me."

"What's that?"

"I've been thinking about your hairless pussy ever since I first saw it. I want you to spread out before me and stroke your luscious lips and clit until you orgasm. I want you to let me watch you come."

That was something she'd certainly not expected him to ask. She'd never masturbated for an audience before. But the thought of being a bit of an exhibitionist thrilled her. She felt wicked just imagining his gaze on her as she pleasured herself. "Okay," she agreed. Her voice was thick with her arousal.

Heart racing, she crawled onto the bed. Obsidian came up behind her as she bent over and nipped her buttocks with his teeth. She yelped. He helped her stack pillows behind her and knelt on the mattress between her feet as she settled.

"I've imagined you on this bed ever since that first night."

"You mean when you stabbed me with your foil thingy?"

"Don't remind me of my foolishness. I *am* sorry for that. At any rate, I would rather have stabbed you with something else," he promised.

"Me too," was all she could manage. Obsidian's hands had come around her ankles, nudging and spreading her legs wide. Never in her life had she felt so exposed. His burning yellow gaze seared her as he stared at her exposed femininity.

"You're wet and ready for me."

How could she not be? This was the headiest, most erotic experience she'd ever had. For a moment she faltered, growing shy.

"Touch yourself. Stroke your flesh and imagine it's me doing it," he demanded. His tongue moistened his lips, and his gaze never strayed from her wet heat.

With little breathless pants she obeyed. Her hands trailed down her body, pausing to tweak her nipples. Obsidian's eyes flared up when she did, so she lingered. She plumped and squeezed her breasts, watching with delight as his cock bounced almost in time with her movements.

Slowly she stroked her hands over her body. Obsidian's eyes never wavered and followed the progress of her explorations. Thanking her lucky stars that she was limber, she widened her legs further and heard him gasp. She moved her hands lower, watching him tense in anticipation.

One of her hands went beneath a leg and spread her cunt lips wide for his viewing pleasure. The other moved to her clit, where she massaged in a circular motion with her fingertips. Her flesh was tingling and swollen. Within seconds she lost her shyness, and began to move in rhythm to her strokes.

Obsidian watched the middle finger of her other hand thrust into her wet sheath, and groaned. He'd never seen such an arousing sight. Never taking his eyes from her, his hand moved to his cock and stroked. Timing his motions to hers, he soon felt close to the most explosive orgasm of his life.

Cady moaned and thrashed as she approached her orgasm. Her fingers increased their rhythm, one thrusting deep inside of her, while three others rubbed her clit in circles. Her hips pumped wantonly in time to her movements.

Obsidian suddenly wanted to do more than just watch.

Releasing his cock he moved his head down between her legs. He heard her gasp as he thrust a finger in alongside hers to feel for her G-spot. Darting his tongue out he licked her, long and hot. Her fingers stopped moving as he slurped her clit into his mouth. He pulled back.

"Don't stop," he commanded. She obeyed, zeroing in on her clit once more. Obsidian's tongue worked around their moving hands and within seconds she was moaning and thrashing again. He felt her flesh spasm against his mouth as she came, and sucked on her hungrily. He thrust two fingers into her, stretching her, feeling her contractions.

He'd never felt such a consuming need for any woman as he did for her in that moment.

With a deep throb in his heart, he realized he wanted to make her feel just as moved. He decided to take it slow and tenderly this time. To imprint himself on her in such a way that she would never forget him. Never forget this night.

No matter what the future held, tonight she would be his.

Chapter Eleven

Obsidian moved up and over her. Their eyes met and held for several heartbeats, speaking volumes. No words were needed between them. They understood each other well enough without them.

Very slowly Obsidian lowered his lips to meet hers. He kept the kiss soft. Made it an exploration of the senses. A rediscovery. He learned the taste and feel of her mouth, and savored her as she deserved.

After what seemed like hours his lips left her mouth and traced the contours of her face. Her golden skin was warm and soft. He was reminded once more of caramels, and darted his tongue out for a taste. It was hard to hold back, but somehow he found the strength.

Cady wondered at his sudden change in demeanor. Until now he'd always been wild when they came together. Though she liked his unbridled, dominant nature, she found this soft side to be just as sexy. His body weighed heavily on hers, taking her down into the mattress. But instead of being threatening, his weight was sweet and protective.

Cherished. That's how he made her feel. Hands touched and teased her naked skin and discovered her every secret. Lips brushed against her so lightly they felt like a whisper. Teeth nibbled at her earlobe, and she sighed.

"Do you like that, love?" His whisper breathed hot into her ear. The light laving of his tongue followed it teasingly.

She could only moan in response.

Hands came between them and cupped her breasts. Her body arched into his palms, thrusting her more fully into his grasp. Fingers kneaded the full globes then moved to pluck at her nipples. With every pull and tug of those fingers, Cady felt an answering pulse deep inside her womb.

Suddenly he pulled back. Before she could voice a protest, however, he tugged and pulled until she lay on her stomach. She sighed when he pushed her braid aside and laid his lips against her neck. It felt deliciously sinful.

Teeth suddenly sank into her shoulder and she squealed. Instinctively she knew he did it to brand her, and eased when he laved the pain away with his tongue. His hands roved over her lightly, raising goosebumps in their wake.

It was all Obsidian could do to keep from ramming into her on the spot. With her back curved and the plump globes of her buttocks rising in the air, his control was dancing a razor's edge. She smelled fresh and sweet. Ready for sex. The taste and feel of her were even better.

He let his hands fall to her buttocks. They were plump and round, lush and soft. She had the juiciest ass he'd ever seen. He absolutely loved a woman with a big ass. His fingers dug into her, squeezing and parting her cheeks. Seeking the puckered flesh between them, he couldn't resist a moment longer.

He buried his face in the cleft of her ass, ignoring her shocked gasp. He licked the sensitive flesh between her cheeks, darting it daringly into her asshole. Growling now in his passion, he lifted her against his face with his hands still at her rear. Raising her in such a way made it easier for him to move down to her cunt. He licked one of his fingers and gently inserted it into her. Then his mouth moved down to her slit.

Cady was shocked and stunned. No one had ever touched her this way. It was incredibly erotic to feel him tonguing her while squeezing the globes of her ass with his hands. She felt dominated when he lifted her, bowing her back. Her head was weighed down into the pillows. Submissive, she eased her protests to let him have his way. When his finger slipped into her she moaned and couldn't help clenching against the delicious torment.

His tongue delved between the folds of her cunt as his finger moved gently in and out of her ass. Never in her life had she felt such a need to be taken. To be owned completely and utterly. It terrified her, but thrilled her all the same. She imagined how it would feel to have his cock inside her the way his finger now penetrated her and flew straight into a violent orgasm.

Obsidian felt her ass muscles clench when she came and twisted his finger inside of her. He knew it would make her orgasm exponentially more powerful. Her scream into the pillows was more than enough reward for his efforts. She was a goddess in her release, more than worthy of his worship. He would have done anything for her in that moment.

After she went limp, spent after her body's release, he reached to the bedside for a condom. Within seconds he was sheathed in the lubricated latex. He felt a moment's sadness to know there was a barrier, however thin, between her flesh and his. But as much as he wanted it, he couldn't leave her unprotected this time. He might lose control, which was something he'd never even come close to with any other woman in all his life.

With gentle but insistent hands, he raised her hips once more. He positioned himself behind her, rubbing the head of his cock against her wetness. Then he entered her. Slowly, inch by inch, until he was seated to the hilt. She was tight and hot around him. He began a gentle rocking motion in an out of her sheath.

Cady sighed, feeling him stretch her over and over. His hands were on her waist, guiding her movements, keeping the pace slow and easy. She buried her face in the pillows, the linens cool against her flushed skin. With desperate hands she clutched at the covers, spasmodically opening and closing her fists as he rode her.

Her pussy made wet sounds as he rocked in and out of her. The only other noises in the room were those of their ragged breaths and the stirring of the mattress beneath them. A full, tingling ache washed through her and unbelievably she started climbing toward another peak. Tears leaked from the corners of her eyes and the feeling swelled until her heart ached with it too.

For a long, long time he rocked against her. His cock filled and stretched her but every time she reached the point of orgasm he stilled. His hands would soothe her until she came down from the peak, and then he would continue his thrusts. He was killing her with the exquisite pleasure.

It felt like hours had passed. Cady's flesh felt heavy with her need to orgasm. Sweat poured from their bodies, making their skin glisten. Suddenly Cady heard Obsidian groan and felt him increase the pace of his thrusts. One of his hands came around her to caress her clit, while the other slipped a saliva-moistened finger into her ass again. She was lost.

The orgasm was so violent she thought she surely must have loosed her bladder on him. She could feel a gush of wetness washing out from her, and realized she had actually ejaculated. Even though she'd heard and read about female ejaculation, she'd never believed it existed.

Now she knew it did. Most assuredly it did, and it felt glorious.

Obsidian must have felt the same because he roared and proceeded to pound into her with the force of a battering ram. Seconds later he shouted again and Cady felt his pulsing orgasm through the condom he wore. He continued thrusting while he came, making her already sensitive flesh scream with the exquisite torment.

Moments later, he pulled free of her and turned her to face him. He kissed her mouth long and sweetly. "Thank you for that, my love," he said before moving down, laying his head on the pillows of her breasts.

"Tryton and the tour of our city can wait a while yet. I'm claiming this time with you for myself," he growled, nuzzling her nipple contentedly. In the next breath he was deeply asleep.

Seconds later, she too fell into a deep slumber with a smile on her lips.

* * * * *

Obsidian slowly awakened to the feel of a hot, wet mouth suckling on his cock.

His hands were buried in the silkiest hair imaginable. Groggy and fresh from sleep, it was all he could do to keep from thrusting deep within that mouth. As it was he couldn't help moving slightly against the pulling, sucking lips. It felt far too wonderful to resist.

Soft, skilled hands played with his testicles, testing their weight as the mouth moved tirelessly upon him. He groaned and thrust tentatively deeper into the hot recesses, careful to keep his movements gentle lest the erotic torment cease. A deeply satisfied moan came from the throat that was working on him, vibrating his cock from crown to base.

With a hoarse shout he buried his fingers deeper into silken hair, and let his passions overtake him.

How much time passed, as he lay there in the delicious waking dream, he couldn't have said. But the mouth was so skilled, so wet and hot, that he couldn't have staved off his orgasm no matter how hard he'd tried. With a hoarse shout he spurted his semen into Cady's throat.

He felt her swallow it down.

Obsidian's eyes flew open. Cady was just licking away the last drop when he flung them both from the bed. She didn't have time to savor the sweet essence of him before he forced a finger down the back of her throat. His movements were swift and though she tried she couldn't fight him off.

"Cady! Baby, oh baby, what have you done?" His voice was a panicked roar as he bent her over with his fingers still down her throat, trying to make her spit up what she'd ingested. "No, please by Grimm, *no*," he roared.

"What are you doing?" she demanded when she managed to pull his fingers from her mouth. "Are you crazy? Most men prefer women who swallow."

"Oh Cady, *baby*," he kept repeating. His voice was ragged and Cady realized it wasn't from anger. But from fear.

"What is it? What's wrong?" She was starting to get worried, too. Instinctively she knew Obsidian wasn't the type of man to ever display fear. But his eyes were full of anguish and terror, plain for her to see. What had she done that was so wrong?

"Please spit it up, Cady." Uh-oh. He'd never said please unless he was being sarcastic. The begging, pleading tone in his voice struck a cold shard of fear into her heart.

Obsidian's voice shook. "You don't understand. *I'm so sorry*. I should have told you why. This is my fault. *My* fault."

"What? Tell me what the hell is making you look at me like that!" she yelled. She had to. His voice had become a roar as he repeated the same words over and over.

"Oh baby, I'm so sorry. I've poisoned you. Please, for Grimm's sake spit it out. Spit it out!" He was shaking her as he yelled the command in her face.

"Poison? That's the most ridiculous thing I've ever heard. Its just sperm, for crying out loud."

"I've told you I can't share my sperm with you. It is against our laws to share fluids, and I couldn't tell you why for fear that you would turn from me in terror. My sperm is poison to your kind, Cady."

"But how can that be?" she asked, though he was too far gone in his panic to answer.

"Why did you have to do this? You're so stubborn, I should have known you would do this. Please, please.... I can't bear it. Do something...*anything*! Just get it out of your system."

Suddenly she felt a coldness creeping outward from her middle. Her entire body felt as if it were freezing. As if her heart was pumping snow through her veins instead of blood. The sensation swept through her, making her knees buckle so she fell. He held her, kept her from falling, but she knew it wouldn't have mattered. She felt the hand of death close in on her...and it was like ice.

"It...it's c-c-cold," she managed before swaying bonelessly in his arms.

"No, baby, oh no. Please stay with me." His voice sounded choked. Like he was crying.

"D-don't be...s-s-sad. Not...your f-fault," she stuttered. Her teeth were locked against the cold. She wanted to reach out and touch his face, to reassure him. Comfort him. But her vision was black, and her senses were failing. Her muscles wouldn't respond.

The last thing she heard before the darkness claimed her was Obsidian's shouts for her to stay with him. And his last roaring cry of...

"Tryton!"

Chapter Twelve

"Obsidian, let her go. Let her go, I've got her." Tryton's voice was calming. He tried to pull Cady's body from Obsidian's clinging hands. "I can't examine her if you don't let go."

"Please save her, for I cannot. She cannot be allowed to die," Obsidian whispered as he rocked Cady's still form.

Tryton's eyes were dimmed with regret. "I don't know if I can save her. But I will try."

With effort Obsidian released her. Tryton gently lifted Cady's small nude body and laid it upon the bed. "How did she...?" Tryton's question trailed off.

"She swallowed it. I...I was asleep and when I woke up...she swallowed it. I tried to make her gag it up but it didn't work. Then I called for you." Obsidian thanked all the gods that ever were that Tryton had heard and arrived the second his shout had faded from the room.

Maybe it would make a difference. Maybe Tryton could save her.

Tryton seemed to sense his thoughts. "I will try to save her. I don't know...no human has ever survived. It's why we've forbidden unprotected sex. Thank goodness humans have invented better condoms than we used to employ in my youth. Until these new latex condoms there were often accidents with our own designs.

"Goodness knows we probably should have just outlawed sex between our races. But human women have always been drawn to us, and we to them. With careful practices there are few risks to our partners, and much pleasure. No Shikar has ever slept or long-term mated with a human woman, though. Not like this. It makes the game more risky. Usually once or twice with a willing human is enough."

He kept talking to fill the void of worried silence. Obsidian was shaking and looming over the bed. It was all Tryton could do to keep from ordering him from the room as he bent and examined Cady. He ran his hands down the length of her, trying not to notice how very womanly her curves were. No matter that everyone saw him as a relic because of his age. He was still a man.

Cady thankfully still had a pulse, though it was very weak. Tryton had witnessed the emotional bond that was already forming between Obsidian and Cady. He had harbored no illusions, and had known this day would come eventually. In fact, he'd counted on it.

He hadn't guessed that she would ingest it orally this first time. He wished it could have been otherwise. It complicated things quite a bit, as the poison could move more quickly into her bloodstream this way.

"Cady isn't like any other woman. She's different," Obsidian choked out.

"She is," Tryton agreed. "And perhaps that difference will be what saves her. We shall hope and see."

Cady's body suddenly thrashed on the bed, startling both men. Where before she had been so still she'd seemed dead, she now shuddered and writhed on the mattress. Her muscles visibly contorted and trembled, and they could hear her bones popping and grinding.

They watched, stunned, as her body reshaped itself before their very eyes.

Just as suddenly as her violent movements started, they stopped. Her bones realigned noisily. A long exhalation of breath escaped her lips and then…silence.

Tryton quickly checked for her pulse but found none. He felt a wave of frustration suffuse him. It wasn't supposed to end like this! How could all his suspicions be false? How could all his careful planning fall to ashes like this? He'd been so *sure* that she was one who could survive a Shikar mating. That she would open the door to new possibilities between their species.

The unmoving, eerie stillness of Tryton's disbelief must have registered to Obsidian.

"No!" he cried and dove for the bed. He started pumping her heart, performing the human ritual of CPR that he'd learned on a lark during a month of leisure from his post. Pumping her chest, then breathing in her mouth, over and over. It was all he could do to keep from screaming his rage and anguish.

He'd lost her.

There was still so much he wanted to say to her. So much to learn about her and have her learn about him. Something big, something altogether new had been shared between the two of them. More than sex, more than partnership, it had been the start of a deeper bond. Obsidian had felt on the brink of a discovery with Cady. Now it was too late.

Tears streamed down his face as he worked her heart and lungs. His arrogant pride was forgotten and he began to choke on his sobs. Never in his life had he known such a sense of loss. His heart was torn in the wake of it.

Forgetting all sense he stopped CPR and took hold of her shoulders and began to shake her forcefully.

"Don't you dare die on me!" He shouted it over and over, shaking her until her head lolled limply on her shoulders.

Tryton was shocked at Obsidian's loss of control. Seeing his friend's emotion for the woman sent a wave of guilt washing through him. He knew enough about Cady through his spies on Earth to see she was far too stubborn to ignore a warning about fluid exchange. If Obsidian had told her she couldn't have his seed, then Cady would have been hell-bent to get it.

Tryton realized he should have warned Obsidian to ignore the unspoken law that humans must not know their Shikar secrets. He should have warned Obsidian to tell her outright why she couldn't—mustn't—take his seed.

But he hadn't warned Obsidian. He had wanted to see the results of this mating for himself, should it come to pass. In his pride and arrogance he'd thought Cady wouldn't be susceptible to the poison as other humans were. He'd assumed that because of her Shikar abilities she would survive, and perhaps even desire a long-term mating with Obsidian. It was possible. The Council had discussed it on many occasions, though none had tried to test their theories.

He was shamed at his actions. The cost for his folly was Cady's life.

But...

Another thought occurred, and hope surged through him. "I'll be back," he promised Obsidian, though Tryton doubted the distraught warrior paid him any heed. He disappeared from the room in search of the one man who might be able to save Cady.

The Traveler.

* * * * *

Obsidian looked up from where he cradled Cady's lifeless body. He hadn't even realized he was alone until Tryton reappeared with The Traveler standing still and calm at his side.

"Give her to me Obsidian."

"No. I won't let you take her to the other side." He gathered her closer to him.

"She is a mortal. In death, her spirit is already on the other side. This is just her empty shell now. Give her to me so that I may find a way to call her spirit back." His voice was a deep pool of soothing calm. It lulled and coaxed.

Obsidian would have none of it. He resisted. "Leave me in peace to mourn her before you take her from me. What possible difference can it make?"

The Traveler's hand rose and pushed back the cowl that, until now, had always shielded his features from other Shikars. "All the difference in the world, warrior. All the difference."

Obsidian's yellow eyes widened in recognition. Every Shikar, from the time they were old enough to toddle to the portrait hall, knew that face like his or her own. "Grimm. But...how..."

"There is no time for explanations, my friend. Please give Cady to Grimm. He will do what he can to bring her spirit back to us." Tryton's eyes were weary from the night's ordeals.

Witless with his surprise at seeing a five-thousand-year-old legend, Obsidian could barely nod his assent. He didn't fight when Grimm reached out to take Cady from him. Could only watch, dumbstruck, as Grimm sat in a chair with her body cradled in his arms.

Grimm reached and put one of Cady's fingers in his mouth. Obsidian had enough wits about him to grow concerned. "What are you doing?" he asked and saw Grimm remove her finger, which was now coated in glistening blood.

Grimm's black, starlight-speckled eyes met his. "I must have some of her blood. It will be easier to hunt her on the other side if I know her taste and scent. There are many souls there. It would take ages to find her without this small bonding."

"What is a small bite when compared to her life? Calm down, Obsidian. Be quiet for a moment," Tryton commanded.

Grimm turned back to Cady. Bending low by her ear, his long blood black hair shielding them from view, he breathed in deeply of her scent. Holding it in his nose and lungs, his mouth full of the taste of her, he rose and brought the woman back to Obsidian.

"I will return," he promised and disappeared from the room.

Chapter Thirteen

The realm between life and the afterlife was one Grimm knew all too well. He often walked here amongst the wandering souls who paid him no heed, seeking solace in the quiet void. Here he could move freely, anonymously, and without worry of keeping his guard up. In this realm no one knew him, or cared about who and what he was.

This was the only place he'd ever truly been able to relax.

Countless forms wandered about here, paying each other no mind. None of them even really knew where they were. They were concerned with only one thing. Finding their way to the other side. Whether to reincarnation, Heaven, Valhalla or Hell, depending on their religion and choices in life, these people were searching for their just rewards.

Sometimes Grimm liked to help them find their way.

He couldn't make them see him, not really. But he could lure them in the right direction. Being a Traveler, no realm was off limits to him. He'd seen the milk and honey lands of Heaven, the fiery pits of Hell, and the great stone halls of the Viking gods. These he'd seen and hundreds more. All the secrets of the universe were his to be had because of who and what he was.

Even so, he was not happy. Was never happy. His existence was at best a lonely one.

The blessed emptiness of this in-between place pulled at him. Lured him to let loose his mortal coil and be free at last. It was always this way. A constant struggle against giving in and seeing where fate would take his scarred soul. He was tired of wandering alone.

Something solid bumped into him. He stumbled back and fell flat on his back.

"I'm so sorry. Here, let me help you." A voice as pure as the spring rain spoke to him from out of the bleak void. "Did you hurt yourself?"

A woman. Dark blonde hair, cornflower blue eyes and an enchanting, adorably crooked nose. But how could this be? She could see him—and he her. In this place, earthly forms held no meaning. Everyone here, save himself, was just a non-descript moving vapor in the darkness.

How could this be?

"You can see me?" he asked. He'd risen from his fall and he looked down when he spoke. She was tall for a woman. Her head reached to just below his shoulder. She tilted her face and regarded him curiously.

"Of course. This is my dream, after all. I control who and what I see. You're very beautiful you know. I'm glad you're just a dream because if you were real you'd knock my socks off." She reached up and brushed back a long lock of hair that had fallen over his face.

"You can't see me here. It's not possible." He tried to ignore the stab of lust and hunger he felt when she touched him. Her delicious scent, of some wild exotic flower, intoxicated him. His cock grew heavy and hard.

"Of course it is. I'm asleep and dreaming this whole thing," she said. Her voice was smooth as honey with a drawling accent he couldn't quite place.

He couldn't resist reaching out to brush softly against her breast with the back of his hand. She was certainly bewitching, though why he should let it affect him he couldn't say. Her nipple quickly grew to a point and she rubbed back against him sensuously.

"That feels really good."

"I can make you feel even better," he promised. He leaned down from his greater height to press a soft kiss against her lips. She moaned into his mouth and it was all he could do to keep from pouncing on her right then and there.

"This is turning into such a delicious dream," she said, pulling back slightly. He let her, though it was difficult. Her babbling continued. "I hope I wake up soon though because I think I'm still driving. I remember driving home from work and then…this dream. God I hope I haven't been asleep long." Her voice was starting to sound puzzled.

It suddenly dawned on Grimm why she could see and talk to him. She was here by mistake. It obviously wasn't her time. He didn't know how she'd managed to keep her physical form in this realm, or how she'd managed to stay cognizant of her surroundings. To his knowledge, only Shikar Travelers were able to accomplish such a thing.

One thing was for certain. She didn't belong here.

With regret, he realized he had to send her back. Now. "Go back to your waking world, human. You don't belong here just yet. Go back." He deliberately coated his voice with his power. Compelling her to obey.

Her eyes took on a glazed, hypnotized quality. "You know something? You remind me of someone."

"It's not your time, you must go back," he stressed, seeing her fight the compulsion.

"You...you look like..." Her eyes drifted shut and her form flickered. Then disappeared without a trace.

Grimm watched her go with a feeling of loss. After a long moment he came back to himself with a jolt. With great effort he remembered his quest to find Cady. Dutifully he pushed aside the odd connection he'd felt with the strange woman. Now was no time for dawdling. He must find Cady.

Breathing deeply of the still air around him he caught a faint trace of her scent and followed it.

* * * * *

"He's not going to make it."

"Have a little faith, Obsidian. These things take time, I'm sure."

"It's been an hour. I don't care if he is the legendary Grimm, he's not going to make it. It's *impossible*."

Tryton sighed, watching Obsidian pace the length of the room again. He hated to admit it, but perhaps Obsidian was right. Never before had this sort of thing been attempted. So perhaps it *was* an effort in futility. Even Grimm was known to fail sometimes. It wasn't often, admittedly. But perhaps this was one of those times.

"Why hasn't he returned?" Obsidian roared the question.

"I don't know. He will return when he's exhausted all hope. Give him a little more time."

As quick as a blink Grimm stood over the bed, looking down at Cady's lifeless body.

"What happened? Did you find her? Where is she?" Obsidian's questions sounded more like accusations in his state of near panic.

Grimm didn't acknowledge him. He simply sat next to Cady and took her hand. He softly called her name. "Come toward the sound of my voice, Cady. Come back."

Several moments passed. Not a sound was made beyond the gentle murmurs of Grimm's voice as he continued calling for her.

Then suddenly, there was a long inhaled scream. Cady jerked and bucked on the mattress, the inhuman wail still sounding from her. With a violent movement she rose from the pillow, and would have launched herself from the bed if not for Grimm's interference. Everyone stared, stunned, as Cady quieted.

All was still but for her rapid breathing.

Obsidian was the first to find his voice. "Oh baby, you're all right." He moved to sit beside her and took her from Grimm's steadying hands. He enfolded her in his arms, thanking all the Gods that ever were for the miracle he'd just witnessed. "Open your eyes, let me know you're going to be all right."

Long black lashes fluttered then shot open. Every one of the men gasped and started. Obsidian couldn't find his voice, but Cady suddenly could.

"So The Traveler *is* the Grim Reaper. I knew it!" she rasped out, voice harsh as if from misuse.

None of the men could find the will to speak. They could only stare as Cady blinked up at them…with her Shikar yellow eyes.

* * * * *

"I can't believe I'm even having this conversation. What you're telling me, essentially, is that Obsidian's sperm has changed me? Infected and poisoned my DNA to the point that it mutated into that of a Shikar?"

"I'm only guessing, but that *is* how it appears. Only time will tell," Tryton said.

"Your reflexes are faster, and you're stronger. I could tell that much, at least, when you struggled against me upon waking. And your eyes are no longer your human brown. What other traits you have inherited remain to be seen. Suffice it to say you are not a human anymore. If you ever were completely human, which I doubt," Grimm pointed out.

"But I don't want to be changed! I want a normal life. I have a job, a car, and a home. I'm not going to leave all that behind. I'll just wear contacts and remember to move really slowly so people can see me."

"It's not that easy, love." Obsidian's voice was coaxing, gentle. "What if, like us, you blister in the sunlight? What will you do then?"

"One word. Sunscreen. Well maybe two more, *Ozone 70.* That's supposed to be the highest SPF on the market."

The three men seated around her looked on in confusion. Cady rolled her eyes. "Never mind. You guys sure know a lot about human products when it suits you," she said thinking of Obsidian's stash of Trojan condoms. "Forget it. Maybe I'll just wear long sleeves and pants all the time."

"It won't work. Don't you think we'd be doing that if it did?"

"I don't want to be a Shikar," she wailed. "I want to be me. Just me...well maybe ten pounds lighter but *that's* it. *Carajo*, I just want things to stay the way they are."

"Well, things may not have changed too much. But in the meantime might I suggest that you avoid direct sunlight altogether. Just in case. Tonight, after the sun sets, you should go home and gather what necessities you'll need until we can sort this out." Tryton tried sounding diplomatic.

"I'm bringing Squaker and that's non-negotiable." She tried and failed to steady her voice. Fear was something she never liked dealing with, and this whole situation was freaking her out.

"Who's Squaker?" all three men asked in unison.

"My cat. And he's coming with me."

"Squaker is most welcome. We also have our animal friends. I think Desondra has two cats—Persians actually," Tryton mused.

"Who's Desondra?"

"She's Zim's wife, a warrior from the Hunter Caste. They don't live far from here, perhaps a league. You'll meet them, and many others soon. Obsidian still has to show you about the city. And some of our women have come together to make you a suit of armor. I hear it's a stunning creation."

"A suit of armor? Are you kidding? I've never needed armor before. Besides it's too clunky. And none of the men wear armor. Why do I need to?"

"You don't have the added benefit of foils, as we do. But you can judge for yourself its usefulness when you see the suit," Obsidian said. "You don't have to accept it, though much work was put into the design."

"Hey, don't go trying to make me feel guilty. It won't work. I've been through a lot today without that added burden. Is it even today or tonight or *what*? How long was I gone?"

"It's late afternoon on Earth," Obsidian answered.

"Shit. I've missed work. I didn't even get to call in. What if someone goes by the house looking for me? They'll think...well hell, I don't know what they'll think. They never know what to think of me. I guess if I'm going to move down here, though, I'll need to say goodbye to the townspeople or they might worry. They've known me my whole life."

"We'll worry about that later, love. Let it go for now," Obsidian urged.

"Yes, you need to rest. Later, after sunset, you can retrieve Squaker and whatever else you need. Only time will tell what changes this night's business has wrought on your physiology. For now I suggest you take things slowly," Tryton instructed, and rose as if to leave. "Let us go now, Grimm. And leave these two to their rest."

Grimm rose, but paused before leaving. His cowl was back about his face, hiding his features in shadows. "I cannot stress to you the importance of keeping my identity a secret for now. I hope I can count on the both of you to keep this knowledge between us."

"I can't help but wonder where you have been all these long years. I certainly hope you will tell us someday. For now, until you give us leave to speak, we will keep this in strictest confidence," Obsidian promised for both of them.

"Perhaps I will share the story with you, someday. But not for a little while yet," Grimm said.

Cady watched Grimm turn and glide into the sitting room beyond, and was suddenly moved to say something to him. She raced after him. "Traveler, wait."

Grimm stopped, hand upon the door handle, and turned to her. "Yes?"

Cady could only think how strange and still he always was. He was such an odd duck. "Thank you. For saving my life."

"Perhaps you will grow to hate me for it in time. This is a new life. Nothing like what you had before." Dark as death, his voice never ceased to give her pause.

"No. I won't hate you. And I won't be scared of you, though you've totally blown my mind tonight. Just thinking about what you did—bringing me back from the dead—freaks me out. But you know what they say, 'Don't fear the reaper.' So I won't. Thank you for saving my life, reaper man." She grinned.

"You're welcome, little warrior." From the shadowed hood, his eyes flashed. Cady would have sworn he was grinning when he turned and left. She stood there for several moments, thinking back over the night's events.

What would happen to her now? Was she really all that different? Glancing into a mirror on the wall she could see the bright amber luster of her eyes glinting back at her. It was an uncomfortable sight, so she looked away almost immediately.

"Come to bed, baby. I'm sure you need to get what sleep you can." Obsidian was suddenly at her side, stroking her hair. "You scared the hell out of me. Don't ever die on me again."

Cady laughed, though it was a weak effort. She *was* tired. "I'll try my best."

"I never want to have to go through that again. I didn't think you would make it back." He seized her suddenly in a rock-hard grip. "Never scare me like that again." Then his lips were on hers.

Ever since she'd awakened from the dark void of her death, she'd noticed how hypersensitive her senses had grown. Before, Obsidian's kiss had drugged her and flooded her body with tingling heat. Now it stole her mind and made her see stars. *God, how good would sex be now?* She couldn't help giggling over the thought.

Obsidian pulled back. "What's so funny?"

"Nothing. I'm just so glad to be alive." She kissed his chin. "Thank you for not being mad because I ate your come." The words made her giggle again. What an odd thing — to fear ingesting sperm — though it was perfectly normal because he was a Shikar. Still, it sounded strange when spoken of aloud.

"Oh I will be mad, when you've rested and recovered. In fact, I'm thinking of spanking you. Being punished is probably the only way you'll learn. I told you my coming inside of you was impossible, that it was against our laws. But you wouldn't listen."

"I thought it was to discourage having children. I thought swallowing was okay. I sure as hell didn't think it was going to kill me," she said defensively.

"It doesn't matter. I *will* spank you, and you will remember to always heed what I say. Now, let's go to bed. Worrying over you has worn me out completely."

Later, as they snuggled beneath the sheets, Cady asked, "Does this mean you can come inside me now? Now that I'm a Shikar?"

Heat radiated from Obsidian's body as he curved it spoon fashion around hers. "Yes." His voice was husky. His cock was already hard against her rear. "But not right now. Just let me hold you." He kissed her hair.

"Yes, please hold me. As tight as you can." Cady yawned and drifted off to sleep.

"I'll never let you go," Obsidian vowed, before he too succumbed to slumber.

Chapter Fourteen

Cady woke up, face down over Obsidian's thighs. "What the hell?" she exclaimed. What was he doing? She was naked, so her ass was bared to his gaze. One of his strong, large hands was rubbing over her appreciatively.

"You need to understand that what you did was wrong and that I was terrified for you." His voice was soft, full of gentleness and a touch of regret. "I can't let you be so foolish as to put your own safety at risk like that. I have to protect you from yourself, and this is the only way I know how to get your stubborn attention." *Smack!* His hand rose and slapped down on her ass.

"Arrrrggh! *Hijo de puta*...you son of a—" *Whack!*

"I'm only doing this to impress upon you the importance of following my orders. You knew better than to tempt fate last night." *Slap!* "You knew better than to disobey me."

"Screw you. You didn't tell me sucking you off was forbidden. Let me up or I'll kick your ass, so help me God." The swats to her rear didn't hurt so much as they humiliated. Her face was red with indignant anger. She struggled to rise, but his hand—the one not presently paddling her ass—pushed her head back down toward the floor. Her rear end was pointed skyward, growing red she was certain, as he continued his punishment.

Smack! "Don't." *Whack!* "Ever." *Slap!* "Put yourself in danger like that. I couldn't bear it if you hurt yourself because of me ever again."

"You're hurting me now you—*you big jerk*!" she stuttered. For the first time in her memory she couldn't find a smart-assed remark to express her displeasure. As soon as she could wriggle away from him, she was going to kill him!

"I'm not hurting you, we both know that." His hand had ceased spanking her. Now it rubbed lightly over her red, abused flesh. It was arousing, no matter how she fought against it. Within seconds she grew wet, and his fingers inserted themselves between her legs. She remembered her anger and squirmed against him. Arousing or not she wasn't going to forgive him so quickly just because he was petting her now.

"If you don't let me up I'm going to shoot you the first chance I get," she swore through gritted teeth.

Slap! "Don't take that tone with me. Before I let you up you have to promise me that you'll never disobey me again."

"Fuck you."

Smack! "I'm doing this for your own safety. I love you, and I don't want anything to happen to you simply because you're too stubborn to follow orders. I'm trying to save you from yourself."

"W-what?" Her mouth was suddenly dry, and it wasn't entirely because his fingers had once again insinuated themselves between her legs. "What did you say?"

"I'm saving you from your own stubborn nature," he said, fingers finding her wet flesh.

"No, the other, you dolt." *Whack!* "Ow! Stop that! Did you or did you not say that you love me?"

"Yes, I love you. Even if you are a smart-assed, stubborn human. I love you, and I don't want to see you hurt ever again."

"Let me up."

"Will you promise to obey me in the future?"

"No, I don't obey anyone but myself." *Smack! Slap! Whack!* "Aaaaaah! Okay, okay. I promise to obey you. *When* we're on the battlefield," she hastened to add.

Obsidian was silent for a moment, and since no more blows landed on her ass, she was inclined to believe he was thinking on her offer. It would be meeting her halfway on the whole 'follow my orders' thing, but it was all she was willing to agree to. Her rear was tingling, and much as she would have fought against admitting it, she was getting horny as hell.

The thick, hard ridge of Obsidian's erection stabbed her in the hip. She wanted to rub against him like a cat. He seemed to sense her growing excitement, and thrust a long finger into her wet sheath. She opened her legs as much as she could to give him easier access.

"Very well then, it is agreed. On the battlefield you will obey my every command, no questions asked. And in the privacy of our chambers I will try to make an effort to explain any…suggestions I might have there."

"I get to decide whether or not to obey you, though. On the battlefield and in the bedroom."

"Only in the bedroom." He was adamant on that point.

"Deal," she said after a moment of thought.

"Deal," he repeated. "Now, I find I am in need of relief. As part of your punishment for last night's debacle, you will see to my needs first." With those words his

127

finger came out of her dripping flesh. Cady saw him lick his finger clean as she rose up and settled astride him.

Their eyes met for a moment then, quick as a blink, Cady pulled back her fist and socked him in the mouth. "Don't ever treat me like that again. See to your needs indeed. You're lucky I'm willing to have sex with you at all after the way you just treated me," she said as he fell back onto the mattress.

Obsidian sputtered and tried to rise, but Cady held him down. There were advantages, she was quickly discovering, to having great strength.

"Cady," he began in a warning tone, but he forgot what he'd meant to say as she fully sheathed him in her wet and welcoming body.

"What?" she said, knowing full well how dazed he was. Lucky for him she was horny as all get out and needed him now. She was still more than a little peeved over the spanking, but willing to let revenge go in lieu of sex. "Cady, what?"

"Nothing. Love me." His words were spoken on a groan.

"I do love you," she vowed, knowing it was true. She did love him.

Slowly she moved on him, rising up until he was almost free of her, then lowering back down. He was so deep at this angle, brushing against all the sensitive nerve endings inside of her. Stretching and filling her until she didn't know where her body ended and his began.

With a ragged sound, Obsidian rose up and popped a nipple into his mouth. His hands moved around to squeeze and spread her ass cheeks as she rocked against him. It was deliciously wicked, the way he seemed to wrap himself up in her.

Dazed, Obsidian felt her hot, wet flesh tense and squeeze around his cock. Unable to hold back, he lifted and bounced her, coming into her harder and faster. She was so wet she was soaking his balls, and he thanked his lucky stars that he'd found so responsive a woman.

He bit and suckled her breasts. Licked and laved her from throat to nipple, bathing her with his mouth. His fingers kneaded the flesh of her rear, moving her on him faster and faster. The keening wails escaping her mouth echoed in his ears and in the room around them.

"Ooooooo, it's too much," she screamed with the overwhelming pleasure. Her muscles clamped down on him. She could feel it, like a rippling fist in her vagina. Shuddering and moaning she came, heart pounding, senses reeling. Her stinging ass cheeks only heightened the erotic feel of his fingers squeezing her, and her breasts bounced as he sucked on them.

"You're so fucking sexy when you come for me, baby," he growled around her nipple. He pounded into her a few more delicious times. "I'm coming too, Cady. Take my seed. Every last drop," he commanded.

Cady was still in the throes of her multiple orgasms, but she felt him when he stiffened against her. She felt the hot wash of come as it flooded her already soaking wet sheath. Every burst from his cock filled her with a kind of giddy joy, and she screamed. Somehow the hot feel of his come managed to heighten her ecstasy, flooding her body with a warm and glowing bliss.

"Oh my God!" she screamed, shuddering over and over against him.

Obsidian only groaned and gathered her tighter against him, still thrusting deep. He knew what she was feeling. Shikars always felt their partner's orgasm along with their own when they indulged in unprotected sex. It was a bond that became more and more addictive each time they mated. He knew for certain then that Cady was no longer human.

She was a Shikar woman in every way.

Almost blacking out from the exquisite torment that wracked their bodies they collapsed back against the bed. They moaned and rocked together, still locked together in release. It was almost half an hour later before they regained their wits.

"Damn! Now *that* was good sex," Cady laughed and snuggled down onto his chest.

Obsidian couldn't have said it better himself.

* * * * *

"I am not wearing this."

"It will protect you. Aren't you glad it's not the clunky body armor you envisioned? You'll have freedom of movement as well as almost impenetrable protection from neck to toe."

"Oh, *hell* no."

"Cady, you are the most stubborn woman I've ever had the misfortune to meet. Several of our women spent three days and nights working to prepare this for you, and you quibble over how it looks. You *will* wear this and be grateful for it." Obsidian's voice had grown diamond hard during his speech.

It didn't intimidate her one bit. "This is worse than Cat Woman's body suit. You can see everything, from my nipples to the crack of my ass. No way."

"You will wear this or you will not be allowed to fight the Daemons anymore."

"Oh yeah? You think you've got the balls to start some shit with me? I'd like to see you try and stop me," she shouted, practically stomping her foot in indignation.

"Nice outfit," came a voice behind her, and she started. Edge and Cinder stepped into the room without so much as a by your leave.

"That looks very…um…very nice, Cady," Cinder said, taking in her appearance with an appreciative look in his yellow eyes.

Obsidian sent a dark scowl in his direction and Cinder immediately backed away with a sheepish grin. "Regardless of how it looks on you, Cady, this suit can save your life. No tooth or claw can penetrate the material. There are retractable blades sewn into the wrists, and secure straps throughout for the guns you seem to fancy so much. It's durable, easy to clean, and it will keep you cool or warm, depending on the weather. You will wear it."

"I look like a dominatrix." She did. From throat to ankle she was encased in a black, latex-like material that clung to her body like a second skin. How the Shikar women she'd met upon receiving the suit had known her measurements she couldn't guess. But here she was, standing in a room of three men—each looking at her like she was a piece of pie—in the most revealing outfit ever made.

Blush? Her? Surely not.

Obsidian ignored her comment. He turned to face the other men. "You have a report for me, Edge?"

"We've found the back door. It's in the middle of a large expanse of woodland. A massive oak has been uprooted from the ground, probably during a storm, leaving bare an entranceway into some underground caverns. It's a large area but Tryton has assigned some Travelers to investigate the area. We're sure its what we've been looking for."

"Make sure everyone is on alert duties tonight. Send more men to guard the Gates, and stand at the ready near the backdoor in case some Daemons manage to get past our Travelers."

Cinder and Edge both immediately left to see Obsidian's orders carried out.

"I'll wear this for now, Obsidian, under one condition," she said through gritted teeth when his attention turned back to her.

"What is that?"

"That I help the women design a new suit. One not so...sex-fiendish."

"Fine," he conceded. "But you get to explain to them why you're not happy with this one."

"That's not a problem. I'm not shy or anything."

Obsidian laughed. "You, of all people, fail to see the irony in your statement."

Cady cocked her head to the side, thinking. Then she blushed and swore. "Shit. Okay, so I'm shy when it comes to being an exhibitionist. But not when it comes to running my mouth."

"Thank you for the clarification. Now, you've donned your weapons for the evening? Good. Let's go get your cat." The smile never wavered from his lips. He took her hand.

One moment they were standing in Obsidian's bedroom, the next they were in the middle of hell.

Chapter Fifteen

Smoke engulfed the interior of her house. Flames licked and ate at the walls of what once had been the only safe haven in her life. "Oh no, oh *no*!" she wailed.

"Cady, grab what you can so we can get out of here." Obsidian had to yell to be heard over the roaring of the flames.

Her grandparents' house burned around them as she hurried to do his bidding. Thankful that Obsidian could just disappear them out of harm's way when the time came, Cady ran through the house gathering her favorite belongings. Despite her pain over the loss of her house, she tried to look on the bright side. At least she had another home to go to. Not many people would be so fortunate.

Moving with preternatural speed, she grabbed a pillowcase and emptied her jewelry box into it. Followed it with her grandmother's precious signed copy of Gone With the Wind, and her grandfather's pipe. On her bed she found her brother's stuffed giraffe and shoved it into the pillowcase with all the rest.

Hurrying through each room, darting between smoke and flames, the pillowcase was soon full of the precious possessions she wanted to save most. Thankfully with her newfound speed and quick reflexes, she'd had enough time to glance about each room in search of Squaker. She'd found no sign of him. She hoped that the resourceful tom had escaped out of his pet door when the fire first started.

"Let's go, Cady," Obsidian called. She rushed to his side, just as the roof caved in around him. She screamed and clenched her eyes shut.

And opened them outside in the yard.

"I am so glad you can Travel," Cady said fervently.

"Me too," he agreed, watching the flames licking at the house. It gave a loud groan as more of the ceiling collapsed. "I wonder what caused this."

Now that the adrenaline had started to leave her, Cady's Daemon hunting senses awakened.

"Look out!" she cried in warning. Dropping the pillowcase she whirled to face the Daemons that emerged from behind the house. They charged at Cady and Obsidian like crazed bulls.

One monster hit her like a freight train, tackling her to the ground. Obsidian moved to pull the foul beast off of her, but was waylaid by the second Daemon. Not one to waste time waiting to be saved, Cady quickly struck out, sinking her fist into the squishy chest cavity. As strong as she was now, it was a simple matter to grasp the creature's heart and tear it clean from the ribcage. Striking out with her feet, she launched the creature off of her and into the air.

In the meantime, Obsidian had engaged one of the Daemons, using his foils to impale the beast repeatedly. One clean swipe of his foiled arm took the creature's head from its body. Slicing downward he cut the creature's body in two, at the last reaching out and taking the still beating heart before the halves fell to the ground.

Still holding the heart of her fallen foe, Cady's hands shook from the adrenaline surge that had washed through her during the fight. With effort she regained control, and realized the heart was still beating. She needed to burn it before the other Daemons found them. She could sense them, and they were very close. It wouldn't do to have the monster she'd just felled rise back up to join the fray.

"*Carajo*, why is it so hard to kill you guys?" she muttered darkly, searching the tiny pockets of her suit. "Obsidian, I can't find any matches."

No sooner did the words leave her mouth than three more Daemons came out of the darkness. They snarled and howled in their guttural language, fanning out to try and surround Cady and Obsidian. Their eyes were bulging and gummy, yellow like a Shikar's but very bloodshot. Skin as black and slimy as an oil slick graced their hulking, brutish forms. Their hands were larger than a basketball and sported wicked, ten-inch claws.

Cady knew from experience that their claws were razor sharp.

One of the beasts closest to Cady drew nearer and roared in her face. Growing angry she roared right back, startling the creature. The Daemon crouched, balancing lightly on the balls of its clawed feet. The creature seemed to grin, displaying its long, dripping fangs.

"*Man* that's nasty. Invest in a toothbrush for crying out loud," Cady quipped and drew her Glock 28 handgun. She fired it straight into the Daemon's face. Cartilage and bone sprayed in a mist as the creature fell back with the force of the shot.

Obsidian sprang at the other two Daemons, as Cady fell upon the other. The monster's claws came up to rake themselves down her back, but fortunately the bodysuit prevented major injury. She would be bruised but her flesh wouldn't even bear a scratch.

Still holding a Daemon heart in one hand and her gun in the other, she beat the monster's face with the butt of her gun. "You like that don't ya, bitch?" she raged down at him. Knowing the Daemons' groins were as susceptible to pain as any other male, she drove her knee into the unprotected area. The monster screamed and tried to buck her off.

With a growl of frustration, she freed one hand by tossing the heart to the ground beside them. It was a simple matter for her to sink her fist into its chest and remove that heart as well. It took effort, but she pulled away from the grasping hold the Daemon still had on her and went to help Obsidian.

Not that he needed it. She could only watch on in fascination as Obsidian whirled and danced between the two creatures attacking him. His foils winked from his arms and legs as he twirled and leapt, slicing his opponents to ribbons. A moment more and Obsidian came to a graceful stop. The Daemons' bodies fell to gooey pieces around him.

"That was totally gross," she said, though she couldn't prevent a stab of green-eyed jealousy over his seemingly effortless skill.

"Perhaps, though still effective. Are there any more nearby?" His foils retracted back beneath his skin.

"No. I think they were just an ambush. How did they find where I live? They've never been smart enough to hunt me down before."

"I don't know. But we must inform Tryton. You are no longer safe in the mortal world. The Horde knows you for what you are now. Even if you could pass through the daylight, you can't go back to your former life. It's too dangerous."

"I know you're right. *Mierda*! I hate this. They're getting more organized in their attacks. Smarter. I don't like it, not one bit."

"Neither do I. Come on, let's burn the hearts in the flames around the house." Just then one of the creatures stirred. It launched itself at Obsidian, taking him to the ground. It was the first monster Cady had felled, and even wounded as it was, it managed to draw blood with a blow from its claws. Blood welled from deep furrows in Obsidian's arm.

Cady rushed to pull the creature off. She heard Obsidian's arm break as the beast struck out at him again. Obsidian didn't make a sound, but Cady knew it was bad. The sound of the crunching bone had been loud, even amidst her hollering and flailing at the beast.

Crunching…munching…chewing. The sounds ran together in her head as she remembered the sounds her brother's body had made when the beasts had gnawed on his bones. The noises echoed in her memory, like a horrible chant from hell.

Her vision turned red. Her eyes burned in her skull like red-hot coals, and with her newfound anguish serving as fuel she found the strength to pull the Daemon away from Obsidian's body. She fell back, with the Daemon in her arms and let the anger ride her like a tide of flame.

*Flame…fire…*a roaring heat suffused her whole body. She couldn't physically contain the wash of pure energy and instinctively pushed at it, muscles going taut. With a sweet gush of relief the power surged out of her, sending the monster flying from her grasp.

A roaring wave of flame washed down the Daemon's body, completely engulfing it. The creature screamed, thrashing about trying to beat out the fire. All of its desperate efforts were futile. In less than a minute the body was reduced to ash upon the ground.

"Did you *see* that? Oh my God, did you see? I totally whaled on that guy's ass! Woo hoo!" She made to give Obsidian a high five, but he only looked at her upraised hand with puzzlement.

"You are an Incinerator. I had heard the rumors, but didn't believe them."

"Believe it, buddy," she laughed. "Though, I'm sorry to say, I can't just do that on command. That's only the second time I've ever been able to do that."

"That's not an issue. You have the gift. Cinder can teach you. He teaches some of the younger members of his Caste. I'm just shocked to know you can do it. You're not like any other human I've ever met."

"Former human," she laughed. "And don't you forget it. C'mon. Let's get these other guys thrown into the fire. I'm hungry and we still have to find Squaker."

"Former humans are an odd race. How can you think of food at a time like this?" He bent and despite his injured arm easily lifted two of the bodies that still littered the ground.

Cady moved to grab a piece of burning timber, using it to set fire to the bits of Obsidian's Cuisinart victims. No *way* was she carrying that filth to the fire. "Well what do you expect? Most people, including me, would normally barf at the thought of eating right now. But I'm too hungry to let it get me down. The last meal I ate was at lunchtime yesterday."

"Why didn't you say something earlier? You came out here without seeing to your needs first?"

"Quit swinging your arms like that or you're going to hurt yourself worse," she warned.

"My arm will heal, faster than you after the spanking I'm going to give you. Are you completely without sense? What if your hunger had made you too weak to fight? You don't take good enough care of yourself." His voice rose over the last in his frustration.

"Put a lid on it, Sid. Help me find my kitty and then get us outta here. I don't want to have to look at my home burning any longer. I'm going to miss it. I had some really good times here," she sniffed. Tears filled her eyes and she blinked them furiously away. "At least no one got hurt. Well, besides your arm, sorry. You can lecture me later. I'm learning it's one of your favorite things to do, and who am I to begrudge you your happiness?" With a cheeky grin that warred with her swimming eyes she jaunted off, calling for her cat.

"Woman, you will never bore me," Obsidian chuckled before following her.

Chapter Sixteen

"So you're saying that this cavern, this backdoor, isn't really a cavern at all. It's an underground lair as large as the entire town at *least*?" Cady was stunned.

"Essentially yes. Somewhere in this lair, though we haven't pinpointed it yet, is a gateway into the world of the Horde. When we find it, we can seal it off. That should reduce the number of Daemons making it to the surface, if not ending the threat entirely," Tryton informed the group.

The six of them—Cady, Obsidian, Cinder, Edge, Tryton and Grimm—stood gathered around the fireplace in the great stone drawing room. Cady tried not to notice how each man's eyes lingered over her breasts and lower belly. It was too embarrassing to dwell on.

She vowed to start work on designing a new suit first thing tomorrow. How hard could it be, really?

"How will we find this gateway?" Obsidian asked.

"I've assigned a dozen Travelers to map out the area. We should have some clue about its location in a week. Maybe less, it's hard to guess."

"How did it get there? There aren't many caves in this area, and what very few you can find are really small. Too small to even stand up in."

"We think it's been dug out by the Daemons. Probably a storm came through and made the job go faster by uprooting the tree at its entrance," Cinder said.

"There was a tornado, a really big one, actually. The first night I saw one of the Daemons it tore through the town, leveling most of the houses in my neighborhood. That was just over fifteen years ago." Cady shuddered.

"We must find and destroy this gateway. There's no telling how many Horde minions have already escaped through it. I won't allow any more." Tryton was every bit the noble leader as he spoke. For the first time Cady could truly see the fearsome Shikar warrior beneath his proud façade. If she hadn't known him better, the unforgiving sight would have chilled her to the bone.

Everyone bowed respectfully to Tryton's command before withdrawing to their chambers. Dawn had broken on the surface. Their duties would wait until the next nightfall.

"I had your belongings taken to my chambers. Squaker is awaiting you there as well, and I had one of the wives feed him when we brought him in. You have been given your own apartments, but I would prefer you move in with me," Obsidian said, placing his hand lightly on her back.

Cady snorted, thinking of the traitorous tomcat's instant liking for Obsidian. The cat hadn't even come to her call when she'd spotted him in the woods beyond her property. He'd sent her a sly look of calculation before launching himself straight into Obsidian's arms. Cady's only consolation at the desertion of her dear pet was the look of shock and discomfort on Sid's face when the cat had settled in his arms and gone to sleep.

Cady snorted. "You don't sound like you're asking me. You sound like you've just decided that's how things are going to be."

"Do you have a problem with that? I thought you would prefer having easy access to my body all hours of the day and night. I would hate to think you were in need and suffering all alone in your bed," he teased.

"You are one egotistical Shikar, Sid. What makes you assume I would even think about you while all alone in my bed?" she quipped.

"Oh I just know you would. You would think of my hands running over your body. Of my mouth tasting all your secret places. Of how my cock stretches your pussy tight when I thrust into you. How my body dominates yours." He bent low, murmuring his words into her ear as they walked through the great stone halls.

Damn, he excited her! Hoping he wouldn't take note of it, she started to walk faster.

"Your hand would reach down and stroke the wetness between your legs, imagining it was my hand. You would rub your hard little clit but you would find no real satisfaction. Your breasts and cunt would tingle with frustration, no matter how you tried to ease the ache. As much as you would hate to admit it you would crave the taste and feel of me.

"Nothing can substitute the reality of how thoroughly I can claim you. You're so stubborn you would deny yourself rather than come to me for relief. I'm only thinking of your welfare, my love."

They reached his rooms. The door clicked shut behind them and Cady launched herself into his arms. She wrapped her legs around his waist and held on for dear life, before planting her lips on his.

"You make me so hot," she groaned into his mouth.

"I've been looking at your luscious ass in that outfit ever since you first put it on. I've been hard all night, wanting you." His hands squeezed and kneaded her posterior. He lifted her and rubbed his erection against the juncture of her thighs. It was more than easy to feel him through the thin material of her suit.

"Help me get this thing off." It was all she could do to keep from screaming in her rising excitement.

"I'm going to make you come so many times you can't walk straight. You're going to be so hot and wet that you will soak the sheets. And then I'm going to lick and suck you until you're even wetter."

"Oh yes. *Yes!*" she squealed into his mouth.

Somehow they managed to unzip her suit and peel it from her shoulders. Underneath she sported a black lace bra, and Obsidian licked her nipples through the flimsy barrier. "You have the sexiest body I've ever seen. So soft and curvy. I could feast on you for years and never grow used to the effect you have on me."

"Please hurry," she begged shamelessly.

"I'll hurry this first time, baby, to ease you a little. Then I want to ride you slow and deep for the rest of the day. I want you to be a useless puddle by nightfall."

Oh lord, she was a useless puddle *now*. She loved it when he talked to her like this. The rest of her suit was removed and Obsidian unfastened his trousers. He carelessly let them fall to the floor around his ankles. His fingers reached down between them, tugged aside her black lace thong, and positioned her wet cunt over his erection.

With a long, hard thrust he rammed himself home. Cady felt his balls bounce beneath her as he came to rest.

The force of his invasion left her breathless and stunned. He filled her so deeply! She was stretched so tightly that she burned.

"Oh yes. Use your muscles to squeeze me just like that, baby. Oh you're so tight and wet." He groaned and began bouncing her up and down on his hard pole.

"Oooo, ooooo..." was all she could manage, moaning and keening as she was impaled over and over. His hands squeezed and parted the cheeks of her ass, and she felt one of his fingers stroking the flesh between. She wailed and thrust her breast up to his seeking mouth.

He sucked on her nipple through her bra, and turned them. With barely restrained violence he shoved her back against the door and pounded into her. "You're so wet and hot, Cady. Can you hear the sounds our bodies make when we fuck? That's one of the things I love about you, your cunt never wants to let me go. It clings to me, slurping out loud when I pull back. And your skin slaps against mine whenever we move. It's like music to my ears." His words were growing harsh as he fought for his control.

She moaned and thrashed her head. Tightening her legs around him she tried to move even harder against him. The angle at which he penetrated her brought her clit into grinding, exquisite contact with his pubic hair. Her fingers dug into the heavy muscles of his shoulders and back, as she held on for dear life.

The door behind them was a thick, heavy wood. But it shuddered on its hinges nonetheless with the force of their mating. Within seconds her body shuddered, the deliciously deep thrusts forcing her to the brink of orgasm. "*Me estoy viniendo.* I'm coming," she cried.

"Oh yes, baby, just like that. Milk me with your hot pussy. You're so tight, so perfect." He moaned, slamming into her as she shuddered over him. "Scream for me, baby, yes just like that. I love it when you're wild and loud, scratching my back and snarling at me when you come."

Cady could feel Obsidian's tight ass flexing against her legs as he pumped into her over and over again. He was so virile. So very masculine. It was like making love to a tireless stallion, and heaven only knew he was hung like one too. She grinned at the thought, coming down from the exquisite precipice of pleasure.

Obsidian growled. His balls grew tighter and tighter against her every time he moved. She decided two could play at the whole naughty sex talk game. Languidly, she leaned down and whispered into his mouth. "Fuck me harder, Sid. Come inside and fill me up with your cream. I love how your cock throbs and pulses in me when you come."

His eyes met hers dead on. "I'm going to make you pregnant now, Cady." It was a vow. A pulse beat later he roared his release, shooting his come straight into the heart of her womb.

Feeling the hot wet essence of him fill her up, Cady instinctively knew he'd made good on his promise and wept with joy.

* * * * *

"*Mámame el bicho*, baby. Suck my cock." Cady opened her eyes upon hearing Obsidian's dark voice issuing the sexy command. She had fallen asleep on him, limp and spent after several bouts of strenuous lovemaking. Now she was positioned lower on Obsidian's golden body with her mouth near his erection.

"I want to feel your lips wrapped around me, like you did that night. Only this time I won't have to worry about endangering your life when I come." He grinned, showing off sharp white teeth.

Cady chuckled and licked her lips. She clearly remembered the salty-sweet flavor of him. Her breathing hitched and accelerated in her excitement. Without a word she bent and kissed the smooth round head of his penis, darting her tongue out to flick teasingly at him.

Obsidian groaned and buried his hand into her already tangled hair. He pulled her closer and she let him, wrapping her lips around him. "Ooooo yes, just like that, Cady," he groaned, and tightened his fists in her hair.

Reverently she ran her hands over his knotted thighs, noting how tense he was while holding back his natural urge to thrust into her mouth. She took his cock deeper until she could have gagged on him. Bobbing her head up and down while suckling and licking him, she reached up and pinched his nipples.

Obsidian roared his pleasure at the caress, bucking against her mouth twice before regaining control. "Give me some warning next time, baby. That almost felt too good," he growled.

If her mouth hadn't been so stuffed with his cock she would have smiled. His uninhibited response to her every touch made her feel so very powerful. She used one of her hands to pump him in response, and licked away the drops of pre-come that were her reward. He tasted *so* good.

"Wait, baby, just wait. I need to taste you too," he said. Suddenly he reached down and turned her so her pussy rested at his face while hers stayed near his cock. She felt his long hot tongue spear through her folds, zeroing on her clit. She cried out and sucked hard on the head of his cock.

Before long Obsidian was rocking her body against his mouth, using his tongue like a cock to spear deep within her vagina. She moaned in her passion, humming against his penis, and he growled his response to the stimulation, vibrating her labia and clit. On and on it went, until they were both crazed with lust.

Cady moved to take him even deeper, almost swallowing him. Obsidian roared and thrust a long finger into her asshole. She screamed her ecstasy and moved against him, seeking more of the deliciously wicked torment.

They both came at the same time, with Cady's body clenching and pulsing around his invading tongue and fingers, and Obsidian throbbing and shooting his sperm into the back of her throat.

They fell into a thoroughly sated sleep, sprawled sixty-nine fashion on the bed, mouths still working against each other.

* * * * *

Cady woke up sometime later when Obsidian lifted her and eased the head of his cock into her already lubricated ass. She tensed instinctively, but he gentled her with his hands.

"Let me in, baby. I'll make it good for you. It will be pure ecstasy, you'll see," he coaxed. His hands went around her to caress her breasts and clit. She relaxed back against him and sighed.

"That's it," he breathed. His cock slipped into her easily with the lubrication he'd liberally applied while she was waking up. They were positioned with Obsidian leaning back against the head of the bed holding Cady over his cock. One of his hands left her and retrieved something from the nightstand.

It looked like an enormous rubber phallus, only it was covered in numerous bumps and ridges.

"I'm going to put this in your vagina, Cady. It will stretch you, and feel heavy at first, but don't fight it. Let it fill you. It will feel so good you'll scream with pleasure," he purred, nibbling her ear.

"What is it? A dildo?"

"It's called a *Smyl*...and it *will* make you smile. It is designed to swell and fill your channel completely, conforming to your shape and depth. It has weighted balls inside that will vibrate when we move, with varying intensity. I've heard many of the wives love these. I want you to use it whenever I'm not around to satisfy you."

He positioned it at her slit. It felt warm, almost hot, and made her tingle with excitement. "It's pulsing," she said breathlessly.

"The balls inside its shaft make it do that. You're already wet and dripping, thank goodness. Now relax and feel me as I stretch your body with mine and the *Smyl*."

She moaned and sighed as the *Smyl* filled her up inch by inch. The texture of it was an almost exquisite friction deep in her sheath. Between the *Smyl* and Obsidian's thick cock, she felt full to bursting. Suddenly he began to rock in and out of her ass, while slowly pumping the *Smyl* into her cunt.

Her breasts bounced as he filled her and rocked her. She felt decadently splayed open. Invaded and dominated. Never in her wildest dreams would she have thought Sid's thick erection could pleasure her ass so thoroughly as it was now. And no dildo on Earth would have been as pleasurable a ride as the *Smyl* was.

Obsidian seemed to guess her thoughts and whispered darkly into her ear. "The *Smyl* was invented so that when a warrior was away at battle his woman could find pleasure without going to the arms of another man. We don't tolerate infidelity from our mates."

Cady could only moan as she rode the two cocks stretching her.

"You are my mate now, Cady. I've claimed you for my own. I won't let you leave me, not now…not ever. Do you understand what I am saying?" His movements stilled abruptly so that she could find her wits.

"What if I don't want to belong to you?" she couldn't help challenging.

Obsidian's hand slapped her ass sharply, and then soothed it with a heated caress. "Don't say things you don't mean. You love me. I love you. And I love to fuck you even more than you love to be fucked. You're mine now, in every way."

Why fight the truth? He was right. But it irked her to have to admit it aloud. "Ok. I'm yours," her voice was ragged. "But you're mine too. I'll have to make a masturbator sleeve for you or something so you stay faithful to me."

Obsidian laughed and surged up into her with his cock and with the *Smyl*. She screamed her pleasure, making him feel more powerful than ever he'd felt before. "I have my hand. And you forget…unlike some Shikars, I am a multiple Caste. I am a Hunter and a Traveler. I can come to you any time of the day or night to see to my needs. And yours. Now be quiet so I can see to your pleasure, my mate."

The bed squeaked and groaned as he pounded into her. The *Smyl* vibrated and pulsed deep within her pussy, while his fingers rubbed at her clit with every down stroke. His cock stretched her ass and it was a deliciously wicked pleasure to be filled in such a way.

His teeth bit her shoulder and she wailed with the pleasure-pain. He laved the little bruise with his tongue, never letting up on the rhythm of their hard ride. The room was filled with the sounds of their loving. Filled with the scent of their passion. It drove them both wild.

Suddenly at the foot of the bed, The Traveler appeared.

"Finish your loveplay and meet us by the cavern. The night is almost upon us and we've already found the portal."

Chapter Seventeen

Cady squealed in surprise and reached for the bedcovers to conceal them. Unfortunately the covers had fallen to the floor sometime during their long day of loving. Her legs were spread wide and she knew Grimm could clearly see her pussy filled as it was with the *Smyl*.

"Try knocking on the door next time, Grimm," Obsidian said in a hard voice. He didn't seem too angry though, because he was still moving in and out of her ass and thrusting the *Smyl* into her wet heat. Cady was beyond embarrassed and unable to find words.

"I couldn't resist the lure of your passion. You both present a tempting vision to my tired eyes." He was silent for a moment. Cady could feel his gaze as it burned a path over her exposed body. It was embarrassing...and yet very arousing too.

Exhibitionist? Her? *Nah.*

"I could have stayed invisible and watched you in secret. But I wanted to watch...and know that you allowed it." His voice was as dark and bottomless as always. But Cady sensed he might be a little uncertain.

Obsidian's hand moved up to stroke her bouncing breast. "Would it embarrass you too much, my love? Grimm is an unattached warrior, and as he is Tryton's personal Traveler he rarely has time to seek out a partner in these troubled days. Would you mind if he watched?" He kissed her neck, passionate and coaxing as he continued his thrusts.

Hadn't Grimm seen enough already, she thought? "I don't think it's a good idea, Sid. It makes me nervous," she admitted, voice weak and shaky. It was difficult to concentrate on anything with two delicious cocks filling her.

"I apologize, little warrior. I would never do anything to make you uncomfortable. I will leave."

"No! Wait." She felt sorry that Grimm's feelings might be hurt. He was an odd man, but she was growing to like him as she learned more about him. "I don't know what I want. I just feel like this is strange."

"He won't touch you, baby. That I would not allow. Ever. He will only watch. We all like to watch every now and then, there is no harm in that. Perhaps you would feel better if Grimm were nude with us?"

She couldn't believe she was doing this. "Ok. You can stay if y-you take off your clothes too." She blinked and Grimm had already disrobed.

Cady almost fainted. He was so large! His whole body was big and golden, and heavily roped with muscle. But it was the sight of his cock that shocked her the most. At least thirteen inches long and two inches around, it was bigger than any other penis she'd ever seen.

What kind of woman could take that on and live? Well at least that woman would die with a smile on her face, right?

"Just relax, baby. Let yourself go. Give Grimm a good show so he can find release with his hand."

She lost herself in Obsidian's beautiful voice. He was using some kind of magic power over her, to make her relax. It turned her on tremendously and her breathing hitched. It was easy to fall in with his wishes, to just relax and let his cock fill her ass over and over.

At first she kept her eyes firmly closed, not wanting to be reminded that she had an audience. But as the *Smyl* tingled and pulsed in her pussy, and as Obsidian groaned and increased his pace, she lost her timidity. Her eyes flew to Grimm across the room. He sat in a chair, head thrown back while watching them, stroking his massive shaft with a beautiful, elegant hand.

Cady watched in fascination as Grimm's hand pumped up and down his swollen, blood-filled member. Obsidian reached around and turned her head so he could kiss her long and hot. Her thoughts left Grimm and focused once more on the erotic sensations sweeping through her body.

Obsidian suddenly twisted the *Smyl* deep within her, setting the weighted ball to dancing. She screamed into his mouth and came with a gush of wet warmth from her vagina, soaking them both. Obsidian roared and thrust deep into her ass, filling her with his come.

Their orgasm lasted forever. Twisting them both on a rack of exquisite torture until they writhed, mindless and uninhibited. They gave Grimm quite a show. Obsidian moved them in such a way that The Traveler was afforded a clear view of Cady's wet, puffed up cunt and his cock spearing between the cheeks of her ass. It was a heady experience for all three of them.

Grimm thrust up into his hand and shot his thick white semen onto his stomach at the sight. His eyes never left the glistening rouge of Cady's filled pussy, but in his mind he was imagining the blonde woman he'd met while trying to save Cady. He imagined his hand was her wet, tight flesh encasing his cock. His orgasm was violent and all consuming, as he let his imagination soar.

It was several moments before any of them had calmed enough to think clearly.

"Knock next time, Grimm. I don't want Cady embarrassed again," Obsidian said firmly.

Grimm bowed his head in agreement and immediately disappeared from the room. The sight of his sperm-coated stomach burned Cady's vision after he was gone. The Traveler was certainly sexy, she admitted, but dangerous as hell. She didn't envy the woman who would mate with him. Not one little bit.

* * * * *

"I don't want to wait up here while you get to do all the exploring."

"Cady, you're pregnant. I will not allow you to join in the fighting. I can't believe I let you talk me into letting you come this far," Obsidian said.

"How do you know I'm pregnant? It hasn't been long enough for your sperm to even reach my womb yet," Cady growled irritably.

Obsidian leaned down close to her. "I shot my come so deep into you that my sperm didn't have that far to travel," he murmured into her ear with a wicked lap of his tongue against her.

"Arrrgh! *Para el carajo* — go to hell." She jerked away from him with no little effort. "I'm going down into that pit with you, no matter what you say. I've battled my whole life for the privilege of closing this gateway and ridding my town of the Daemons' threat. Don't take this away from me, Sid."

They stood, toe to toe, for several beats of silence. Then Obsidian's amber eyes softened, and he reached out to lightly caress her hair.

"Very well. You have earned this and more with your feats of courage and bravery over the years. I have no right to take this moment from you. But please remember that I am hard on you only because I wish to keep you safe. Even though I know you're more than capable of taking care of yourself, I still worry about you, my love. I always will." He leaned in to press a soft kiss to her lips.

Cady's heart melted. "I understand, Obsidian. But don't try to smother me, or make me into something I'm not. I'm sure you wouldn't like me half as much as you do if I were the 'stay at home' type. I need to go down into that pit and be where the action is."

"Just please be careful, my love. Be alert and on your guard. I have no idea what awaits us down in the caverns." Obsidian grasped her hands and turned with her toward the black, gaping hole in the earth that had once been the home of the great roots of a mighty oak.

Cinder, Edge and Grimm stood waiting.

"Let's go kill some Daemons," Cinder growled, as flames trickled out from his burning eyes.

"There are three Travelers already awaiting us below. When we begin to close the gateway, the Daemons will be alerted and they will try to stop us," Grimm said, his voice as dark and smooth as the devil's.

"Everyone be ready. The Travelers must not be interrupted as they close the back door. Protect the

Travelers above all else, understood?" Obsidian was every bit the fierce leader in that moment.

As a group they moved forward and descended into the pit.

Chapter Eighteen

It was dark and dank in the hole. The drop from the entrance was no more than eight feet but a small tunnel led them from there, on a slight incline, deeper into the bowels of the earth. Because of the cramped space afforded them, they were forced to crouch as they walked in single file. Within moments a foul stench permeated the air around them. It was the smell of death, both old and new.

How long they descended, Cady could not have said, though it felt like an eternity. Then, up ahead in the darkness, she saw that the tunnel widened. It opened up into a vast underground chamber with dark tunnels that led off in every direction.

"Which way, Traveler?" Obsidian asked softly.

"Follow me. It isn't much farther," came Grimm's black velvet voice from the shadows.

Grimm led them through one of the many tunnels. This one was much larger than the last, and it allowed them all to move about freely. Despite the darkness, they could see clearly in the shadows the overwhelming scale of the underground cavern. It was terrifying in its grand design.

Cady looked about her with a feeling of dread and horror. How long had this cavern been here? Had it occurred naturally, or had the Daemons dug it out over the years? Knowing that this doorway to evil had existed here for years was enough to make her shudder with fear. Could she have hoped to ever discover this 'backdoor' to the world of the Horde on her own? And even if she had, would she have had a chance in hell of closing it off?

Thank goodness for the Shikars, she thought to herself. For all their arrogant ways when dealing with the human race, they were all that stood between the Earth and the Horde. They were all that kept the Daemons at bay.

"Through here," Grimm spoke, interrupting her thoughts.

They passed through a monstrous stone archway and into a great open cavern where three other black-cloaked Travelers waited. Behind them loomed a jagged tear in the face of the stone wall. Despite the darkness surrounding them, the depths of the tear seemed so much blacker and darker, as if it sucked in all the light and swallowed it up.

"Hell is just around the corner," whispered Cady with a shudder of revulsion.

"We will begin the closing now," Grimm said.

The four Travelers moved as one to surround the jagged hole. They raised their arms and began a chant that echoed around the chambers with a haunting rhythm. Cady could not understand the language, though she instinctively knew this was the native tongue of the Shikars. Despite the fact that all the Shikars spoke perfect English while in her company, she sensed it was not their preferred language.

The Shikar race was one of unfathomable skills and power. Cady realized she was only just scratching the surface of their secrets. She looked forward to the years she would spend with them, learning all that they had to teach her. That is, if she lived through *this* night first.

Several moments passed. The Travelers continued to chant in the strange, yet lyrical language of the Shikar, while the others stood and watched. Cady began to wonder if all their caution was for naught, and was almost thankful for the anticlimactic end of the Daemons' backdoor threat.

"Cady, do you sense anything?" Cinder asked in a whisper, moving close to her side.

Cady allowed her senses to flare out, seeking for signs of any threat. "No. I feel only the cold of this place," she answered.

"I hear from Tryton that you are not only a Hunter, but an Incinerator as well. He asks that I teach you to control your fire handling skills. Will this be acceptable to you?"

She looked at him, seeing his glowing eyes burn in the darkness. "I'll look forward to it. Sid says you're the best of your Caste. I want to learn everything there is to know about being an Incinerator."

"I have no doubt that, given a few years, you'll surpass even me in skill," he whispered with a grin. Waves of heat emanated from him, like a blacktopped road in the hot summer sun. Cady realized then how very dangerous an Incinerator like Cinder could be. He was like a slumbering volcano, volatile and deadly when awakened. She wondered if she could ever be as powerful, or if she even wanted to be.

"Silence! Be alert, all of you," commanded Obsidian. "We can't afford to let down our guard, even for a moment."

Cinder moved away from Cady to take his former position across the chamber. Time passed, and Cady was once more lulled by the Travelers' chanting in the darkness. It wasn't hard to imagine that this was a tomb, quiet as the grave aside from the chanting, and dark as the sleep of true death.

Cady didn't remember much from her short stay in the arms of death. Only the great endless void, before Grimm had found her and led her into the light. But what little she remembered of death was reminiscent of waiting in this bleak and foreboding place. She felt swallowed up by the darkness that surrounded her, and soon forgot that there were others around her.

There were only the black depths of the cavern, and the chanting of the Travelers.

Then…the lone beat of a drum in the dark.

Cady was shocked out of her hypnotic state by the sound. She darted a look around to see if the others had heard it, or if it had been a figment of her imagination. Cinder, Edge, and Obsidian each stood at the ready, though they gave no sign that they had heard.

Another lone beat, echoing just beneath the lyrical chants.

"Did you hear that?" Cady whispered, with a pounding heart.

"Hear what?" Obsidian asked.

"N-nothing. Never mind," she breathed. Perhaps she had imagined it. She was growing far too nervous, but she was sure she didn't sense the presence of a Daemon, and that was enough for her to relax. Her peace of mind didn't last for more than a second.

Another beat sounded. And another.

"What the hell is that?" Cady whispered frantically.

"What do you hear, Cady?" Obsidian moved to her side.

"Maybe a drum...I'm not sure." *Boom.* "There it is again." She whirled around, eyes delving into the dark shadows that surrounded them.

Boom. Boom. Boom. The beats were coming faster now.

"I hear nothing, aside from the Travelers," said Edge.

Boom, boom, boom. Boom, boom, boom.

A heavy feeling of terror and dread filled Cady, the likes of which she'd never experienced. "Oh, *shit.* Something's coming—" Her words were cut off as the whole cavern shuddered beneath them.

"On your guard!" Obsidian roared as they all tried to keep their footing on the unstable ground.

Boom, boom, boom. Boom, boom, boom. The sound was deafening.

"Do you hear it now?" Cady screamed.

Obsidian stepped in front of her as a great shadow swept out of the gateway before them.

"What *is* that?" Edge yelled to be heard over the roaring of the trembling earth.

A vision from the depths of hell stepped out of the gateway. It stood at least twelve feet tall, and was almost as wide. It looked more horrendous, more terrifying, than any Daemon Cady had ever seen. Its skin oozed black slime, and its massive teeth were stained husks that curved out from thick, blistered lips. Maggots danced in its eyes, and ropy tentacles spasmed out from its barrel chest and potbelly. Instead of feet, it sported hooves, and its hands were like great spiked clubs that were larger than Cady's whole body.

"It's ugly, that's what it is," Cady yelled back. Though her words were flippant, her heart quailed in terror.

Her words seemed to capture the creature's attention. It moved forward, ignoring the Travelers as if they weren't there. It roared, a dreadful and mighty sound, and charged the Shikar warriors.

Edge and Cinder moved to meet it first. Foils and flames danced around the monster's body in a stunning display. The monster roared again and lashed out at the two warriors with its spiked fists. Both men danced gracefully out of reach, never ceasing their barrage of attacks on the monster.

Seeing that their efforts did little damage to the creature, Cady stepped around Obsidian and drew two guns. She fired over and over, in quick succession. Blood and gore flew as her bullets struck home, but to no avail. The monster was far too strong to be felled by mere bullets.

Obsidian gave a fierce battle cry and launched himself at the terrifying beast. He darted around and scaled up the creature's back, sinking his foils deep into the grotesque flesh of its shoulder and neck. The monster screamed in pain and fury, and flailed at Obsidian. Obsidian drew back then repeatedly struck out at the creature's vulnerable flesh with his foils.

Boom, boom, boom.

Cady heard the resounding noise again. It was coming from the monster, though what it was she could not say. She moved closer to the fray, drawing another gun. The hellish tentacles that graced the trunk of the creature's body drew her attention and she fired directly into them.

The sickening sound of tearing flesh echoed after every shot she fired. With an enraged roar, the monster threw aside Cinder and Edge and made straight for her. A long tentacle darted out and wrapped itself around her ankle. Another and another streaked out and attached themselves to her arms. Her gun went flying through the air as she was pulled in close to the nightmarish creature.

The smell of death and decay assailed her nostrils. She tried not to scream out in terror as she was drawn close to the tentacle-ridden torso of the beast. Struggling and gasping, she tried and failed to escape the creature's hold.

Boom, boom, boom.

Cady heard the drumming sound again. This time she knew it for what it was. It was the creature's foul heart, beating strong in its breast.

Boom. Boom. Boom.

"*Sprig 'ald Horde, daculian. Eprish 'ald Horde, primarsandh.*" The creature's voice was like a terrible scream from the deepest pit of hell. The sound froze Cady's heart with terror.

Her words belied her fear. "Foul beast from hell! Why don't you go back into the pit? There is nothing for you here but defeat."

The monster's maggoty eyes widened at her words. As if it actually understood her. Though Cady knew that was impossible. Daemons were a mindless lot at best. She renewed her struggles to escape, but was struck dumb by what she heard next.

"*Human. Pitiful human,*" the words were a wet and guttural sound, uttered from the monster's own throat.

The Daemon shook her like a rag doll, and roared at the Shikar's. "Sampriss dai humund? Inquit nof' lessind Shikar, drakon'winn humund?"

"Illian nochif lessind humund. Illian septum Shikar!" Obsidian roared in answer and charged the beast.

Boom, boom, boom. The creature's heart sounded.

Cady was tired of being shaken about. She wrenched with her body and shrieked in pain and surprise as her foils breached her skin and tore through the tentacles that bound her. The monster screamed, and Cady launched herself in what she hoped was the vicinity of the monster's heart.

Tentacles whipped around her, but she ignored them as best she could. With the aid of her foils she fought them off and sank her arms shoulder-deep into the creature's chest. The monster fell beneath her, and Obsidian was at her side immediately.

Together they pulled the huge heart free from the Daemon's chest. It was as large as a watermelon, but Obsidian managed to tear it apart in a feat of tremendous strength. The creature screamed and writhed beneath them, but Edge and Cinder kept them safe from harm as they fought off the flailing arms of the beast.

"Cinder, burn it," Obsidian commanded, throwing him the split portions of Daemon heart.

A giant ball of flame licked out of Cinder's eyes and consumed the heart in a blaze. Cady and Obsidian were thrown free as the creature bucked and writhed in a frenzy. Cinder dared to move closer and gave a wild cry as his entire body became a torch, which he used to set fire to the monster's grotesque body.

Within seconds it was over. The monster was destroyed. Its heart and body lay in ashes on the ground.

In the ensuing silence, the Travelers' chanting soothed the weary Shikars. Despite her still exposed foils, Obsidian held Cady close to him after reassuring himself that she was relatively unharmed but for a few scrapes and bruises. Cinder and Edge crouched, still at the ready, should any new threat reveal itself. The Travelers continued, unfazed, to speak the spells that would close the inter-dimensional portal.

Several moments later, the jagged tear in the stone seemed to close in on itself. The cavern wall seemed to heal itself, until no sign of the tear could be discerned. The Travelers had closed the backdoor. The Daemons' threat to Earth was over.

"Are you all right, Cady?" Cinder asked.

"I'm quite alright Cin, thank you."

He laughed. "Cin. I like that. It's so much more masculine and wicked than Sid." Cinder winced as Obsidian landed a blow on his shoulder for his teasing.

"You have shown much courage tonight, Cady. I salute you, warrior woman of the Shikars," Edge said with a show of respect.

"Thank you, Edge. Now…how do I make these things go away?" Cady asked, waving her foiled arms and hands about. The glowing, blue-white blades winked eerily in the shadows.

"Once you relax they will retract. You're like a Shikar child who has just discovered the blades. They too have trouble with their foils at first," Edge answered with a chuckle.

Grimm appeared at Cady's side. She jumped in surprise. The thought occurred to her that she might never get used to the Traveler's uncanny ability to take her unawares. She couldn't help sending him a withering glare at the idea.

"Shall we go home? The dawn is already upon us, and our work is finished here." Grimm held out his hand and everyone stepped forward to take it.

In the blink of an eye they were home.

Epilogue

"Do you think you can be happy here with us, my love?" Obsidian asked quietly.

Cady rolled over in the bed to face him. Thankfully, her foils had retracted as she'd relaxed after her second orgasm beneath Sid's demanding body and the *Smyl*. She was still humming with the afterglow of good sex. "Yeah, I think so. For the first time ever in my life I can be open about who and what I am. I'll miss some people up on the surface of course, but I'd miss you more if I left." She smiled. "First thing tonight after sunset, I'm going into town to say goodbye to a few special people. I'm going to tell them that I'm leaving with my new husband and am unlikely to return. I don't want anyone to worry about me, especially after my house burned down."

"I'll go with you. We'll wear sunglasses to disguise our eyes and make everyone think we're eccentric because of it," he teased.

"Everyone already thinks I'm eccentric. I'll bet that wearing sunglasses at night won't make me seem any more or less weird to them." She laughed.

Squaker hopped onto the bed and meowed plaintively to see there was no room for him in their nude sprawl. He crawled over their bodies, turned up his nose in disdain, and left the bedroom in search of whatever cat mischief he could find. Cady giggled at his antics and watched him strut off.

A few moments later she asked softly, "What did that Daemon say to you earlier, Sid? And what did you say back to it?"

Obsidian sighed heavily. "It's difficult to translate, but what it said was essentially this. 'You have invoked the wrath of the endless army, and you shall die. All shall die before the wrath of the Horde.' Then you spoke to it in your human tongue and the creature realized you were not like us. It assumed you were human. It said, 'stupid Shikars, do you think to hide behind a human woman? Do you think a human can destroy me where you could not?' and so on and so forth."

"What did you say to it?"

"I said, 'You should cower in the face of justice, foul creature. This is no human, but a Shikar warrior queen who will see you pay for your crimes against the people of Earth.'"

Cady kissed him soundly for that. "I knew the creatures could talk, or at least communicate with each other. I didn't know they could stream sentences together like that, though."

"That was not a normal Daemon. I think it was one of the higher-ranking members of the Horde army. I've never seen one so foul, though I have fought against many different Castes of Daemon. I hope never to see one like it again."

"I agree. You know, Sid, I think I need a vacation after tonight. According to you I have a baby in the oven, and I want to concentrate on that for a while. Well, that and your marvelous body, of course," she purred, stroking her hand down his chest.

"Saying things like that will not get you the rest you said you needed earlier," he growled, reaching out to stroke her uncovered breast.

"I'm too wired to rest right now. I think I need something to relax me so I can sleep." She grinned wickedly and let her hands wander down to caress his already swollen cock. A droplet of pre-come coated her finger, which she daringly showed to Obsidian before licking it cleanly away. "Yummy," she teased him with a smile.

"That's it. I'm through playing fair with you," he groaned. In a swift move that left her breathless he threw her legs up over his shoulders and swooped down to lick the seam of the slit between her legs.

"*Ooooo, yes*. That feels so good, Obsidian." She moaned and tightened her legs around his neck, mashing his face closer to her wet flesh.

Beyond words now, Obsidian thrust a long finger into her and slurped her clit into his mouth. While his face was buried between her legs, he pulled and tugged at her sensitive nipples with one hand and finger-fucked her with the other. He suckled on her sweet flesh, using his lips, teeth and tongue to drive her wild. Soon she screamed and bucked beneath him, wild in her passion.

"Come on my mouth, baby," he commanded raggedly. Immediately she obeyed, and through their bond he felt every contraction, every wave of pleasure that swept through her.

When she quieted, spent from her splendorous release, Obsidian rose up and thrust himself balls deep into her wet heat. They both groaned at the suddenness of his penetration.

"I'm going to pump my seed into you until you're full of it. Until you can't take anymore. Then I will bathe you in the tub…and start all over again."

Cady squealed in excitement as he started his deep thrusts. *It's going to be a very long day,* she thought, smiling like a loon.

But sometimes that's a good thing. Sometimes that's a very good thing indeed.

* * * * *

Later that day, as Obsidian and Cady loved each other in their chambers, Tryton and Grimm spoke quietly of recent events.

"She has proven without a doubt that some humans can mate with us. Even better than I expected, their bodies actually change and become like a Shikar's. Soon Cady will learn all the joys of being one of us. She will make a formidable warrior…and mother, may the gods help us." Tryton chuckled at the thought of the fiery woman raising a brood of Shikar children.

"You were right to recruit her, for she is an asset to our army. But now there is the matter of the other open backdoors scattered across the surface world. How the Daemons have managed to get past our guards at the Gates, I still haven't figured out. They are usually too stupid to think for themselves, let alone plan an invasion of this magnitude," Grimm murmured.

Tryton turned thoughtful. "Yes. We must investigate the why before we can end the threat by simply closing their portals. Time, unfortunately, is working against us."

"We will find a way to stop the Horde," Grimm said firmly, determination a palpable thing in his tone and words.

"We must, my old friend. We must prevent the invasion at all costs. Or the Earth will fall to its knees…taking us along with it."

WANTON FIRE

Sherri L. King

Preview

Prologue

They were surrounded by the Daemons; their entire group penned in by the monsters that were supposed to be too dull-witted to accomplish such a feat. But these Daemons...they were different from their predecessors. So very terrifyingly different. They seemed coordinated—a working unit with powers of strategic reasoning and logic—which was surely impossible. The beasts were mindless. They were vicious, evil and cruel to be sure, but mindless all the same, with no powers of higher reasoning. But this group, these seven creatures, had worked together against the three Shikar warriors, hemming them in back-to-back, facing outward against their foes.

The Shikars were tired, beyond exhaustion. For them it had already been a long night of hunting and killing these beasts among the jeopardized Territories of Earth. They'd saved the lives of countless humans this night, but they would not be able to save themselves. Not against these formidable foes. The warriors were breathless, gritting their teeth against the biting pain of their battle-worn muscles and bones, preparing themselves for a last stand against evil. It was all they could do. Their pride as warriors demanded that they stand their ground and face their deaths with courage and valor. They would not go down without putting up one hell of a fight.

The monsters stalked around them, as if judging the Shikars' strengths and how best to attack against them.

Their burning yellow eyes were windows into hell's fire, gateways to the fiery pit itself, seeking—ever seeking—an opening to attack. An unspoken command seemed to pass between the vicious predators. In the next breath, as one, they rushed the Shikars, attacking en masse.

Shrieks of battle and death rang out into the night...then all fell silent.

Chapter One

Hamburg, Germany

"Would you quit that? You're embarrassing me! Just be cool, be real, and you'll blend right in."

"Cady, we've been blending in with humans since long before you were born," Obsidian growled. "We know what we're doing."

"Yeah. Right. Then if you're so damn comfortable out here why are you darting in between cars, ducking into corners, looking over your shoulder every few minutes, and basically appearing like you're a bunch of lunatic criminals? You're drawing far too much attention to us with your antics. *I've* noticed that you're not so great at subterfuge…and so has half of the city!"

"How would you have us act, Cady? Would you have us stand in the middle of the road and wait for an attack from any quarter? Is that what you would prefer?"

"You are such a jerk, Sid. Just be cool, as I said, and follow my lead." Cady sniffed the night air. "Ah ha. Hang on. I'll be right back." She darted across the dirty wet street and ducked into a garishly lit shop on the other side, leaving her group to stand behind and wait for her.

"I don't feel comfortable being out here like this, Obsidian." Edge's smooth voice betrayed none of his nervousness, despite his words to the contrary.

"Neither do I. But Cady thinks we'll find something here. We'll just have to bear with her until she knows more."

"I hate the stink of this place." Cinder scowled. "I much prefer the farmlands we've been frequenting of late. The smell of animals and crops is not so unnatural as...this." He gestured to the passing cars, wandering people, fast food restaurants and nightclubs that lined the dingy city street.

"Do you think I enjoy this any better than either of you? I would much rather be at home playing with my son or loving my woman until she bears me another. But we have a duty here and I'll be damned if we'll go back home before we kill a few Daemons this night." Obsidian looked around with no small amount of discomfort at their surroundings. Cady may be used to frequenting the world of humans—she was a former human after all—but he definitely was *not*. Where Edge and Cinder often frequented the surface world to find willing female companionship, he himself had not often found the time to so indulge himself before meeting Cady, his wife. He was ill at ease here, on the surface world.

He thought back to the meeting between himself and his love...if so tame a word as 'meeting' could be used to describe the cataclysmic effect they'd had upon each other that first night. They'd fought like wildcats, each sustaining injuries from the other, battling for supremacy in those first few moments of confrontation with a tireless fervor. They still warred for supremacy of each other, fighting for the upper hand in almost every situation, no matter how insignificant. Though now instead of ending their skirmishes with bloodshed and bruises they usually ended up settling things in bed.

Obsidian smiled dangerously. He often enjoyed pricking his mate's temper if only to spice up the play in their bed. She was a fiery lover. More than a match for his voracious Shikar appetites. Sex with her was explosive and truly amazing...when it wasn't mind-blowing, tender, full of gentle kisses and soft-spoken vows of love. He would never tire of her. And he would see to it that she never tired of him.

He loved her more than life itself.

And now he had a son, Armand—named after Cady's lost baby brother, the tragic victim of a Daemon attack—thus his heart was full of tender emotions. His son was the image of himself, with his mother's impish smile and mischievous ways. He was perfect. Never in his life had Obsidian expected to be so blessed in so short a time. But now he was a husband and a father...and more than ever he vowed to defeat the threat that could one day snatch those precious things away from him. Cady and Armand were his life. He would protect them with all of his being and more.

Cady emerged from the shop with a sack in her hand. She came to their sides with a slightly smug, yet gamin grin on her face, drawing Obsidian from his inner musings.

"Ta da! Now these will help us appear more like tourists instead of no-good thugs. Ever had a foot-long with the works?"

Cinder laughed. "I always have a foot-long that works."

"Ha, ha. You are such a geek, Cin. I mean a foot-long hot dog—bratwurst actually, I think." She pulled out a cylindrical package of foil and handed it to him. "Try it, you'll like it. It's loads better than your usual Shikar-grown mutton or grain, if you ask me. Ugh. I am getting so tired of eating the same old stuff day in and day out. Maybe Tryton will be willing to import some fast food now and then if I ask." She distributed her treasures to Edge and Obsidian, keeping one for herself, then showed them how best to open and eat the confections without getting the messy toppings all over themselves.

Hot dogs? Cinder looked at Edge and sent him a worried, questioning look. Were they really expected to eat *dog*? Edge shrugged, looking as confused as he felt. Cinder sniffed the food and winced. It smelled tangy and rancid and he was certain that the clear, white topping upon it was inedible. "What is this?" he asked, picking up a piece of the warm, squishy stuff.

"Sauerkraut. It's fermented cabbage. Try it," she said firmly, "you'll like it." Cady took a healthy bite of hers and Cinder struggled not to turn green.

Fermented cabbage? In other words, it was rotten. He'd be damned before he ate anything *rotten*. Cinder smiled and, to please Cady, he took a tiny bite out of the end of his poor, cooked dog. The dog tasted far worse than it smelled! He quickly turned his head away from the others and spat the offensive refuse out onto the street. He held the hot dog behind his back, focused his energy, and burned it to a crisp in his hand. He crumpled the ashes and let them scatter harmlessly on the wind behind him.

Edge sent him an angry look. He would not get off the hook so easily as Cinder had. He had not the skill of an Incinerator. Edge was on his own. Cinder sent him a smug grin and dusted his hands clean of the offensive food.

"You're already finished, Cin? Good grief, you must have been hungry—why didn't you say something earlier? Here, have another." Cady reached into the paper sack and retrieved another of the awful dogs. Cinder tried not to cringe. "See? I told you they were good." She smiled, but Cinder could have sworn that she knew—somehow actually knew—what he had done with the first dog.

Cinder bit back a groan and accepted another foot-long from Cady's hand. Edge chuckled and took a daring bite out of his own...Cinder was surprised when he took yet another, larger bite, after that. Edge was obviously possessed of a much higher tolerance than he for the horrible human food.

"What exactly are we looking for here, Cady?"

"What are we always looking for, Cin? Daemons."

"But here, in the middle of a city? Of all the places they've frequented of late, I haven't heard a tale involving such a populated place."

"And why do you think that is? Any clues? I've often wondered myself why these creatures don't just swarm into a city and take their pick of the humans that wander about here," Cady pressed.

"Maybe psychics only frequent unpopulated areas," supplied Edge, who still munched contentedly on his hot dog.

"Again—why? Don't you ever wonder about these things?"

"No doubt, even as dull-witted as Daemons are, they know better than to tempt fate and discovery by entering large cities." Obsidian sighed, clearly impatient. "But we are not here to question their ways, and to do so will only waste precious time. We are here to protect...and I don't see anyone who needs protecting right this moment."

"Trust me, Sid. I have a feeling. We need to be here tonight. I can just feel it, okay?"

Obisdian sighed and pulled her tight against his side. "We'll stay close to one another and stay aware. You'll let us know when you sense any changes around us, if I don't sense them first." He winked at his wife. They were always in competition with each other now to see who had the strongest Hunter skills. "But I don't like being in so crowded a place. I don't like thinking that a Daemon would dare come here and wreak havoc. I don't like it at all."

"Neither do I," Cady agreed.

The group was silent for several long moments as the human world moved on in ignorance around them. Cinder quickly burned his second bratwurst and scanned the people that littered the streets. Such an odd group, humans. He had little use for them, really. Neither did any of the other Shikars to his knowledge. He only really interacted with them when he needed a woman...or two. He did so love human women. Their soft arms, plump thighs, tender hearts and welcoming bodies were the stuff of decadent dreams. He would have preferred that the human race run itself into extinction as it seemed so wont to do but for the loss of the women.

Cinder was drawn out of his thoughts as Cady went still. Something was amiss.

Cady's breath misted into the air as she exhaled a long, pent up breath. She leaned into the night, swaying out of Obsidian's arms, eyes going heavy and distant. Cinder watched the process with a growing alarm. Cady's strength as a Shikar Warrior of the Hunter and Incinerator Castes grew by leaps and bounds every day. It never ceased to amaze him how powerful she had become...was becoming. He tried to remember what life had been like before she had joined their ranks. She had been a human woman then. She had been an amazing warrior even then. But now...she was the stuff of legends.

"Holy Horde, they're close." Her voice was hoarse, strained.

"How close? How many?" Obsidian demanded.

"I don't know." Her voice broke. "They feel so different. Their presence seems so strong one moment and then just...it just kind of fades away.

"How can that be?" Edge asked.

Cady ignored him. "C'mon. There's something this way."

"How many are there, damn it?"

"I don't know, Sid!" Cady's arms flailed in frustration and her long braid whipped about her shoulders and back. "I'm not even certain what I'm feeling is the presence of a Daemon or something else. But whatever it is, it's strong, and it's this way. So just follow me, all right?"

"On your guard everyone," Obsidian cautioned.

He didn't have to warn them twice. Cinder felt the fire that was always burning just beneath his flesh, begin to kindle and spark. He didn't like this situation. None of them did. But he would see that these humans were kept safe from whatever threat was posed to them, if that was the will of The Elder, Tryton — and it was.

Lately Tryton seemed quite obsessed with humans.

The four of them moved efficiently through the crowded sidewalks until they came upon a thundering nightclub.

"The Desolate?" Edge said, easily translating the German sign that hung above the establishment, the words blinking in bright neon colors that belied the darkness of the name. "Sounds quaint."

"It's an industrial or techno club, I think." Cady looked the place over with a thorough attention to detail.

"What the hell does that mean?" Obsidian asked.

"Industrial and techno are types of music. Very loud, very heavy music with complex beats and such. That's all I know. I was a fan of very few bands in my youth—I didn't really have much time for music."

"Would you look at these humans?" Edge muttered in their Shikar tongue so as not to offend the natives. "They look so somber with their white faces and funeral garb."

"Not all of them." Cinder tried not to gawk when he saw a woman sporting a two-foot high Mohawk in various colors and shades of the rainbow. Her piercing struck Cinder as particularly interesting. She had rings and bars in her ears, eyebrows, nose, lips…she even sported silver studs lined in a row up each alabaster forearm. He'd never seen their like before. She wore a clear plastic top with red dots positioned just over her nipples, and a long red velvet skirt. "Wow," Cinder breathed, unable to tear his eyes off of the spectacle.

"Well. Let's go in."

"Wait. You can't be serious, baby, surely."

"I don't want to go in there any more than you do, Sid. But we have to…that's all there is to it."

Cady produced a thick wad of human currency—Tryton kept them well supplied for their ventures above the surface, though how he obtained the funds was a mystery and probably better left as such—and paid their entrance fees. Cinder walked in ahead of the group, curious about what lay in wait for them in this strange place. They passed through a door into a dimly lit foyer. There, a shirtless man in black latex pants asked them for proof of ID. Cady produced their documents—high quality forgeries procured through Tryton—for the man to view, and they were admitted through yet another door.

Here was a place of thundering, shadowy chaos. Blinding white strobe lights pulsed about them in the dark, revealing in flashes a huge group of undulating human bodies. The Shikars were on the outskirts of a dance floor, swallowed by the throng of people that pumped and swayed to the heady music. Cinder winced. The air was thick as syrup with the noise. It pulled at him like a weight, and every bass-ridden beat of the music thudded in his chest with the force of a physical blow.

"This isn't so bad." Cady yelled to be heard over the din.

"Are you mad? This is horrendous. It reminds me of the Gates...except the air is easier to breathe," Edge yelled back.

"I expected much worse. The DJ is pretty good."

"What the hell are you talking about?" Edge was growing more and more agitated as the music swarmed around them like the thunder of the Horde's giant heartbeats.

"DJ—disc jockey. I wonder who it is?"

"I give up. You've lost me entirely—but I don't care. I can't stay here. The noise, the crowd, the lights...it's all too much. What, by Grimm, are we supposed to find here?"

"I don't know." Cady had the gall to laugh when Edge glowered at her. Cady never lacked for gall.

Cinder looked around them. The place was swarming with humans. It was such a wild and busy place, this nightclub. He'd never witnessed its equal in chaos and celebration...for that seemed what the humans were intent on doing. Celebrating. They drank heavy spirits, kissed and fondled in a sea of damp, tender limbs, and danced in rhythm with the music. He saw them all as they probably would have least liked to appear. Fragile, vulnerable creatures who were not long for the world they so took for granted. A small woman bumped into him, then turned and rubbed her soft, plump body against his. He took her in his arms and undulated back against her, marveling that so small and luscious a creature could approach one as dangerous as he without a care for her own safety.

"Don't stray too far, Cinder." He heard Obsidian call out behind him but was more riveted by the sea of bodies that moved to swallow him up. His partner rose up, pressing her scantily clad body even more firmly against him, and kissed him full on the lips.

Cinder tasted alcohol and amphetamines on her breath, but he kissed her anyway. Her lush, precious mortality clouded over him like a thick perfume. Their kiss ended and Cinder clearly saw in her eyes the invitation for more serious play. But he set her back with a gentle smile and used his preternatural speed to escape without her notice. He was sure she was too inebriated to notice his seeming disappearance. He let the crowd take him deep.

The music had changed tempo but he couldn't remember when. Now it was not so fast as it was thick and plaintive a tune. The lights flashed so that he could find no peace from their invasion, even when he closed his eyes. Men and women alike rubbed against him in a brutal, sexual dance that had his senses reeling. He'd never felt so out of control, so in tune with a chaos that beckoned with the promise of fleshly love and lust even as it bludgeoned him into madness and confusion. Time lost all meaning. The music played on and he was forced to worship it, along with everyone else.

Cinder gasped for breath that did not have the salty-sweet taste of human sweat. He could catch no sight of his group in the flashing confusion, and upon realizing just how long he'd been immersed in this pagan dance, he searched for a way to the edge of the dance floor. He finally broke free and had a moment to look around, to collect himself and his drunken senses.

A flash of pink hair caught his eye and held it riveted. The vibrant hair belonged to a woman, young in form and face. A lovely woman. Cinder could see, even from this distance that she was heavily painted, heavily submerged in the role—whatever it was—best suited to the atmosphere of this strange place.

Her lips were glistening, glittering red, a full and delicious looking mouth. Her large hazel eyes were rimmed in thick black lines, her lashes dripping with similar cosmetic adornment. She wore a tight outfit—a shiny second skin of some strange man-made material—consisting of a sleeveless top, which also left her toned abdomen exposed, pants that rode low on her boyishly slim hips, and chunky-heeled, thigh-high boots. Of all the people in the club, she looked as though the clothes had been made especially for her. She wore them with a negligent style that drew the eye and held it…at least in his case.

She stood on a dais or stage of sorts, bathed in a halo of blue and red lights. She wore a strange headset at her ear as she moved in time to the music. Her lusciously kissable lips were pursed in concentration as she studied the table before her, and the discs that spun upon it. Cinder instinctively guessed that the music mercilessly pounding through the place played forth at her orchestration. She was responsible for the otherworldly tempos stealing through him like a thief in search of his soul.

He couldn't pull his gaze away from her. There was just something indefinable about her, setting her apart from the humans gathered around at her feet. She seemed some kind of pagan goddess as the crowd raised supplicant arms to her, begging her for more, crying out for the music to keep flowing. He'd never seen anything like it in all of his many years as a warrior. He'd never seen anything like *her*.

He stood there for…he couldn't have guessed how long. Minutes? Hours? He didn't—couldn't care. He watched the ethereal goddess orchestrate her music, dance to her music, count out the beats of her music as she changed seamlessly from one song to the next. A singular eternity could have passed and he wouldn't have worried about it, so long as he could watch her.

A green-haired man stepped up from the crowd, moved to her and whispered in her ear. Cinder felt an inconsolable sense of jealousy and loss. The man was too familiar with her. He knew her intimately; he had to for taking such liberties as kissing her on one of her alluringly bared shoulders. He had no right to feel such things for the woman, was foolish to even come close to such a passion for a human. But there it was—he was weak where she was concerned, in a way he'd never been weak before. He wanted to turn away, wanted to leave this crazy place that was filled with temptation and want and need.

But just as he turned, just as he found the strength to walk away from the siren behind the turntable, the music changed. The woman stepped back from her post and flexed her shoulders as if they ached. Pink and black waves of hair danced about her as she jauntily descended down from the stage and disappeared into the throng of people, leaving Cinder to take in the seemingly endless length of her legs as she walked. His heart thundered.

He especially favored women with long limbs…and she had the longest legs he'd ever seen.

A voice sounded over the loudspeaker as the music boomed loud enough to wake the entire Horde. "Let's hear it for our own, incomparable DJ SteffyStealth!" The announcement was voiced in thick German words.

Cinder waited a moment, fighting his impulses, which had become irrationally fixated on the woman…and then followed her through the crowd.

Fetish

Sherri L. King

Preview

Prologue

Aerin looked into the smooth, glassy surface of the pond. She didn't care that the cold, damp of the ground was soaking into the fabric of her serviceable grey skirt. Didn't care that the mud and rocks on the small shoreline of the water's playful edge were scuffing her black leather pumps. Nothing so inconsequential could have mattered to her in that moment. For the first time in weeks she'd caught sight of her reflection...and she was trapped, held riveted by what she saw in the water-mirror.

The face reflected in the depths of the pond was too round, far too plump, and full of too many shameful stresses. The soft, brown hair was straight and unappealing, lying in a bodiless hood over her round skull. Her brown eyes were set too close together, and wrinkled from too much squinting behind her thick-rimmed glasses. Her nose was too large. Her skin far too pale.

Nothing she saw made her the least bit happy to be caught in her own skin.

This was why she never looked into mirrors. Being fat her whole life, being ugly and plain and *boring*, had made her avoid any reflective surfaces like the plague. But she'd never reacted like this, with such self-loathing and pity. Nothing had changed enough for her to recoil so violently to this unexpected glimpse into the pond. Except for one thing.

Somehow, she'd gotten old. On top of everything else, now she was no longer young.

She shuddered, looking at the image of her own hated face. Time had ravaged that face with a brutal, merciless glee. *My god...I'm forty-seven years old. Forty-seven.* Somehow she'd ignored it; until now she'd never bothered to give it much thought. But here the truth of it, at last, struck her like a blow. The salad days of her life were behind her, nothing was left for her now but the routine of tomorrow and tomorrow and hopefully, if she was lucky...another tomorrow.

"I've never done anything spectacular with my life," she whispered into the watery-mirror, suddenly frightened, "I've never been anybody special. Never felt anything," she swallowed hard, "*real.*"

And when had she ever had the chance? A fat, ugly, brainiac nerd like her rarely got any sort of chance for adventure or love or any of what made life worth living. She wasn't stupid; she knew how people saw her. How people always saw her—and all of the others who were unlucky enough to be as physically ill-favored as she.

She was a desk worker. Her world was a relatively safe one, for all of its sometimes cutthroat atmosphere. A world of tight cubicle walls and impersonal colleagues. She was a typesetter at a small printing company, designing and laying out wedding invitations, business cards, letterheads and the like, for thousands of paying customers throughout the region. The job paid well and took no small amount of speed and skill, which was a boost for her ego. But it was also the type of job that required nothing of its workers in the way of personality or looks.

But oh, if she'd been someone else — someone prettier — she'd have done something different with her life. With good looks, she'd have never been so painfully shy, and maybe she would have had the courage to pursue a career as a dancer (which she'd always secretly longed to be), or perhaps an art dealer, or even an entrepreneur. With a svelte body she'd have surely married early in life, instead of reaching the age of forty-seven — *forty-seven* — with her virginity still intact. Or maybe she would have never married at all, but taken many lovers instead, just for the fun and variety of it all.

For the adventure.

She splashed her hand weakly into the pond, breaking its smooth surface into hundreds of ripples that each reflected a perfectly wretched, distorted image of her face. Her *hated* face. She splashed the water again. Fat droplets splattered up as a result, wetting her cheeks so that the water from the pond lingered and mixed with the tears that already drew their tracks down her cheeks. How she hated and loathed her face. Hated and loathed herself. All two hundred plus pounds of herself.

Groaning, she rose clumsily and backed away from the all-too-brutally-honest body of water. The well-kept grounds of the park came back into her consciousness as she tried valiantly to dry her tears and straighten her clothes. Blaming out of control hormones (the dratted change of life was already full upon her and wreaking havoc with her emotions), she strove to overcome the harsh moments before the reflective pool. Hating herself for her weakness, she brushed lingering mud and leaves from her panty hose.

I am no weakling. I am not so self-absorbed that a mere glimpse of my reflection should make me blubber like a baby.

Aerin cleared her throat of the last lingering vestiges of tears. Her thick fingers, trembling, but only slightly, pushed her heavy glasses farther up the bridge of her nose. They had slipped as she bent over the pond, and she hated how they made the tip of her nose itch when they fell low. She hated glasses, period. But her eyes were too damaged for even the most radical laser surgery, and at forty-seven it seemed a little late to even give consideration to contact lenses. She'd been wearing glasses since she was seven years old and would undoubtedly wear them until the day she died.

It was difficult, but she rallied her spirits. It was, after all, Friday. And Friday was her favorite day of the week. The day when she had two whole days of freedom to look forward to. The day when a long, hard week of work was at last behind her. Every week was long and hard. Every weekend was a forty-eight hour period of rest and recuperation, and long hours with books and gardening and quilting. Friday was a boon, her own very favorite day. A transitional day.

Lunch hour was almost over. Aerin's plain, brown-paper-wrapped mayonnaise and lettuce sandwich lay uneaten on the park bench behind her. She had no memory of leaving that bench, only remembered seeing her face so suddenly and starkly before her unprepared eyes. Maybe she'd fallen. Maybe she'd crawled down from that bench, onto the damp ground, towards the water, without even consciously meaning to do it. Compulsive behavior had been second nature for her ever since the first faint signs of menopause had awakened her in the night with feverish hot flashes.

She hoped no one had seen her odd behavior.

Who was she kidding? No one gave her a second glance. More often than not, if they happened to see her, they looked quickly the other way—as if they were ashamed to see such a vision of overweight drudgery. Of course no one had seen her moment of self-pity. They were too busy heaping their pity upon her. No, that was too harsh of her. She was forcing her own low self-opinion onto others, when she had no idea how they really felt about her, when they likely felt or noticed nothing at all.

Aerin hated herself for that, too.

Picking up her sandwich with a disgusted grimace, she started the short walk back to the office. It was a lovely day. Cool and gray—nothing odd there, as this was Seattle and almost every day was like this—but today the song of birds was in the air and the scent of spring was in the breeze. And such a lovely, clean breeze it was.

A piece of paper, blown by that very breeze, flew up and shoaled against her blouse and jacket. It tangled there, trembling for but a second. Long enough for Aerin's clumsy, impatient grab at it. Long enough for her to read the machine-printed words inscribed upon it.

It was an ad for some sort of a nightclub. Nothing unusual. Nothing exciting. But, inexplicably, her heart jumped. Her pulse picked up its pace. And her gaze flew over the text not once, but four times before she could manage to tear her gaze away.

Fetish

*Here every fantasy can be indulged with safety and with care. Be and do everything you've ever imagined. At **Fetish**, nothing is taboo.*

That was it. Only those few words and a local cell-phone number. Fetish. What an interesting and apropos name for a place where 'every fantasy' could be indulged. Her lips twisted. She'd never heard of such a place, of course, because she'd never made a habit of visiting themed nightclubs before. Or any night club for that matter, themed or otherwise.

But...*but*.

Maybe there was a first time for everything. Not ten minutes ago she was bemoaning the long years of her life and the lack of excitement she'd encountered therein. Maybe this was a way she could create some excitement for herself. In a place where, so long as the color of her money was green, it didn't matter who she was, or what she looked like.

It was shameful. It was frightening. But she was forty-seven years old, and so scared of that fact that she'd ignored it until the realization of it bit deep, with enough pain to make her weep. Fright or shame had no place in the thought that maybe, just maybe, Fetish—or another club like it, if this one proved a little too much to take—could be the soothing balm for her unexpected brush with a mid-life crisis.

And after all, it was Friday. The weekend lay before her, along with all its endless possibilities. She clutched the paper in fingers gone suddenly desperate, before firmly tucking the ad into the inner breast pocket of her suit jacket. Her dull, gray, suit jacket.

Aerin winced and hurried back to work as quickly as her thick ankles could comfortably carry her.

About the author:

Sherri L. King lives in the American Deep South with her husband, artist and illustrator Darrell King. Critically acclaimed author of *The Horde Wars* and *Moon Lust* series, her primary interests lie in the world of action packed paranormals, though she's been known to dabble in several other genres as time permits.

Sherri welcomes mail from readers. You can write to her c/o Ellora's Cave Publishing at P.O. Box 787, Hudson, Ohio 44236-0787.

Why an electronic book?

We live in the Information Age—an exciting time in the history of human civilization in which technology rules supreme and continues to progress in leaps and bounds every minute of every hour of every day. For a multitude of reasons, more and more avid literary fans are opting to purchase e-books instead of paperbacks. The question to those not yet initiated to the world of electronic reading is simply: *why?*

Price. An electronic title at Ellora's Cave Publishing runs anywhere from 40-75% less than the cover price of the <u>exact same title</u> in paperback format. Why? Cold mathematics. It is less expensive to publish an e-book than it is to publish a paperback, so the savings are passed along to the consumer.

Space. Running out of room to house your paperback books? That is one worry you will never have with electronic novels. For a low one-time cost, you can purchase a handheld computer designed specifically for e-reading purposes. Many e-readers are larger than the average handheld, giving you plenty of screen room. Better yet, hundreds of titles can be stored within your new library—a single microchip. (Please note that Ellora's Cave does not endorse any specific brands. You can check our website at www.ellorascave.com for customer recommendations we make available to new consumers.)

Mobility. Because your new library now consists of only a microchip, your entire cache of books can be taken with you wherever you go.

Personal preferences are accounted for. Are the words you are currently reading too small? Too large? Too...**ANNOYING**? Paperback books cannot be modified according to personal preferences, but e-books can.

Innovation. The way you read a book is not the only advancement the Information Age has gifted the literary community with. There is also the factor of what you can read. Ellora's Cave Publishing will be introducing a new line of interactive titles that are available in e-book format only.

Instant gratification. Is it the middle of the night and all the bookstores are closed? Are you tired of waiting days—sometimes weeks—for online and offline bookstores to ship the novels you bought? Ellora's Cave Publishing sells instantaneous downloads 24 hours a day, 7 days a week, 365 days a year. Our e-book delivery system is 100% automated, meaning your order is filled as soon as you pay for it.

Those are a few of the top reasons why electronic novels are displacing paperbacks for many an avid reader. As always, Ellora's Cave Publishing welcomes your questions and comments. We invite you to email us at service@ellorascave.com or write to us directly at: P.O. Box 787, Hudson, Ohio 44236-0787.

Printed in the United States
20697LVS00004B/154-213